AGAINST THE GRAIN

I'M DONE PRETENDING

Mandy Hull

For permission requests, write to the publisher, addressed "Attention: Permissions Coordinator" carol@markvictorhansenlibrary.com

Quantity sales special discounts are available on quantity purchases by corporations, associations, and others. For details, contact the publisher at carol@markvictorhansenlibrary.com

Orders by U.S. trade bookstores and wholesalers.
Email: carol@markvictorhansenlibrary.com

Creative Contributor - Jennifer Plaza
Cover Design - Low & Joe Creative, Brea, CA 92821
Book Layout - DBree, StoneBear Design

Manufactured and printed in the United States of America distributed globally by markvictorhansenlibrary.com

MVHL

New York | Los Angeles | London | Sydney

ISBN: 979-8-88581-129-3 Hardback
ISBN: 979-8-88581-130-9 Paperback
ISBN: 979-8-88581-131-6 eBook
Library of Congress Control Number: 2023918926

TESTIMONIAL

"Mandy Hull candidly shares a journey of resilience, depicting the profound depths of personal strength in the face of formidable life challenges. Through the raw and unyielding narrative of overcoming adversity, readers will find inspiration, solace, and a profound sense of hope. A testament to the indomitable human spirit, this book resonates deeply, reminding us that even in our darkest moments, we possess the power to persevere and emerge triumphant."

—Lori Hogan, BA, Psychology

DEDICATION

The auburn-haired eight-year-old sprinkled
with freckles wearing an amazingly mustard yellow,
polka dotted dress as the inspiration
for writing this book.
She was enough then . . . and still enough today.

Mandy Hull

CONTENTS

Mandy Hull

PROLOGUE

Change is constant. My endeavors growing up in western Indiana proved this to be true. Domestic darkness, the rotation of rentals to shambles to unmet essential needs. After acknowledging the abnormalities in my homestead, I felt a calling to rise above it. I became a master at shielding my upbringing from the world as to not get labeled for situations that I felt didn't truly define me. Defying all family odds by going against the grain, I was able to complete a lot of firsts from college to family planning to starting a business. On paper, I had accomplished a lot per society standards but still felt unsettled. Once I began looking within myself and began uncovering all of my concealed emotional wounds, I finally began to feel the well sought after freedom and peace.

My hope is that this story of self-discovery as an adult is an inspiration for others to dive within to learn more about themselves and accept the past as it is.

CHAPTER 1

FOREVER

T ake a deep breath - bring in the golden light - the light of peace . . .

I arrived at the hospital, alone.

The reception desk line wound through to the lobby. The security guard stood next to the metal detector, waving people through one at a time after checking their bags. I forgot about the purse inspection. It prompted an immediate mental review of my inventory. I couldn't think of anything that would set off the alarm other than possibly a nail file. I didn't care if they confiscated it. I needed to get into the waiting room on the second floor nearest the operating room where my sister was undergoing surgery. I wish I knew exactly what it was for, but if it was to save her life, it didn't matter.

I made my way to the receptionist. "I'm here for my sister. She's in surgery. They said on the phone I could go up."

"One moment, please." She typed for what seemed like a full minute, then asked, "Name of the patient, please."

"Holly Carlson."

"Relationship?"

"I'm her sister, Jenna Williams." I drummed my nails on the counter. The anxiety built while I was standing in line and now that I was at the desk, my patience was at the bare minimum. "Please, ma'am. I really have to get up there."

The woman looked at me and frowned. She filled out the name tag and handed it to me in slow motion. Not on purpose. I think that was just her normal speed. "You're all set. Have a nice day."

I took the sticker, pressed it onto my sweater, and hurried down the corridor to the elevators. There was a small crowd hovering next to the buttons. I had to wait for the second round. My phone buzzed in my pocket as the second car emptied. I answered, stepping into the small space.

"Mommy, I forgot to tell you. I got all my spelling words right today!"

"That's great sweetie. I'm so proud of you." The elevator dinged, and the doors opened. I stepped into the waiting room at last. My sister's number was on the overhead monitor. They still highlighted it in yellow. She wasn't out of surgery yet, which meant I hadn't missed the doctors. "Honey, Mommy has to go. Keep up the good work."

"Okay, bye." Zach hung up the phone, clearly content.

It warmed my heart to hear his joy. I worked hard to make sure each one of my children knew I was proud of them. Not just when they excelled, but also when they failed. I wanted to let them know that success is not giving up. You change your strategy or you keep trying until you get whatever it is you're trying to reach. No matter what my heart felt, I wasn't going to pawn those feelings of fear off on them. Children were innocent and should remain that way.

Speaking of children, I sat in the only remaining seat across from a small girl, about eight years old, and a man I assumed was her father. To one side of me was a cocktail table; on the other was an elderly woman who'd fallen asleep. I didn't want to attract attention, so I put my purse on the floor between my feet and took out my phone to check my emails. It was hours since I checked for messages and I was hoping to get a response on a property pending outside of Indianapolis. It was a brick three-story apartment building.

I scrolled through the inbox, deleting the advertisements and spammers. One email stood out. It was from the school's Parent Teacher Association. There was going to be a Mad Hatter Tea Party the following weekend. It was a fundraiser for a coat drive. I'd forgotten about it. I set a reminder to go through the kids' old clothes. I wanted to donate as much as I could. The memory of being on the receiving end of donated clothing has always stuck with me.

I glanced up to see the little girl staring at my bag. I looked down and saw a snack bag of goldfish crackers and a fruit snack peeking out. Her eyes darted to her father when she caught me glance back at her. She tucked her feet under her and snuggled into the man's arm. He put his hand on her head and patted her hair. "We'll get dinner after I hear about Mommy," he said.

Her small lips pulled into a frown, her eyes glistened. Medical knowledge was lost on most adults. I could not imagine what thoughts were going through her young mind. She was just getting to the age of reason. "Daddy, I'm hungry," she whispered.

"I know, now stop." I knew the father didn't mean anything by his statement, but a child does not know how to stop being hungry. They do not stop; they stop talking about it. Their stomachs still ache and grumble.

And maybe I was projecting my own experience onto the girl, but I reached into my purse and pulled out the snacks. "Excuse me, sir. Do you mind if I give these to your daughter? I carry them for my kids. I have extra in the car." I didn't, but I wanted to give him a way to remain humble.

Offering the food could have been mistaken as an act of charity, which may have been unwelcome. It could also mean that he thought I did not approve of his parenting practices. I figured by explaining why I had them and then showing how little I needed them, he may be more apt to oblige the child.

"Thank you, but we taught her not to take anything from strangers. I don't want to send mixed signals." He grabbed the girl's hand and held it clutched to his chest.

The saleswoman in me came out. "That's fantastic. A lot of parents forget about stranger danger. I'm a big advocate for setting our kids up to make the wisest decisions when we can't be around. My name is Jenna, by the way." I smiled at him. "I'm waiting for my sister. She was in an accident and rushed to surgery. I have no idea what's going on in there."

We made eye contact. "My wife's in for hysterectomy. Endometriosis and fibroids. This peanut will be our only child."

"Well, you have a beautiful little girl. You're lucky. There is no guarantee my sister will ever see her children again." I pushed the purse to the side with my foot and crossed my legs.

He shook his head. "Sorry."

I waved my hand. "I have hope it'll all work out. We'll do whatever it takes to get her back to living the life she wanted. The doctors here are miracle workers. I know she just has to be fine." I teared up for real and grabbed a tissue from the side pocket of my purse. "You sure she can't have one? They're not doing me any good."

He looked at the frowning girl. "I guess it wouldn't hurt, bein' that we're here in this situation and all."

"True," I said, handing the two packets to her. "Lucky

for us, we don't have to be in this predicament on a daily basis. I guess we have to look for good fortune where we can find it. There are some who come for regular procedures. I just hope my sister, Holly, isn't one of them."

The father took the packages and opened them for her. She sat back, swinging her feet and humming while inspecting the little red bunny shaped fruit snacks. He held onto the crackers.

It seemed like an eternity since I parked my car and went through the entrance ordeal, but it was only ninety minutes. I wondered how long the father and daughter were here. The girl finished the snacks and took to drawing invisible doodles on her pant legs. Glad that I could help lighten her evening, I wished someone would have been there for me when I needed something to take the edge off the deep pangs of a gnawing stomach.

As a child, our family cashed in the old paper food stamps. We'd buy something cheap, like candy or Kool-Aid packets, so they would give coins back. The more transactions, meant the more change received. We could use the coins for fuel or alcohol—always for something that was not food related. As an adult, I wonder what the store employees thought of minors checking out using food stamps. Gathering around a table to enjoy a meal wasn't the norm in our house. Mom would simply make what she could pull together. Often, I would reach for a

can of vegetables as an entire meal. I learned to appreciate the flavor of unseasoned green beans and cans of corn. It made eating less sodium as an adult easier. It also meant I was not used to eating luxuries such as butter.

Hunger was a feeling I never wanted my kids to experience, let alone other children. Maybe that girl had a full refrigerator at home with clean dishes and drinking water, but I knew better than to speculate. What happens behind the scenes is not always visible on the surface. I knew that from the many domestic abuse calls where law enforcement would arrive to speak with my father for abusing my mother. It was often enough that our parents taught us to manipulate the truth or cover it up for the family to get by. We also learned to lie to the police about our father's whereabouts when he was in hiding. He wasn't far, but we'd say whatever he told us to say. It was better than the verbal and physical abuse that came in torrents when he drank.

He was always drunk.

He was drunk the night he slapped my mother hard enough to leave a welt from his calloused hands. She screamed so loud. I remember him pulling her hair back, her eyes wide and wet with tears. His eyes were lost in the red skin from his alcohol induced anger. It was a special color that struck fear in my older sister, Becky. One night, he threw our mother on the floor and kicked her in the back. She lay there, not moving.

We thought she was dead.

Becky ran to a neighbor's house to call 911. We learned that hope was crossing your fingers. It was such an intentional thought—prayer. We would literally cry out loud that everything was going to be okay. Help couldn't arrive fast enough—it never did.

Praying was a practice I still follow. Sitting in that black plastic chair, I crossed my fingers when I closed my eyes and prayed to God. I asked him to save my sister; to give her back to us. *Dear God, my sister Holly needs this prayer more than I do. I know you have a plan, and I trust in you. But I'm asking if you could answer my prayer and let her come out of this. I'm not ready to lose her, no matter how much we disagree. She's still my sister and I love her. Thank you for all you do. Amen.*

This prayer was so authentic and real—literal—no recitation. It came from my heart.

Not ten minutes passed when the stripe over her number on the screen changed to green. She was in post-op. Not long after that, a team of doctors came in and called me to the consultation room. I kept my fingers crossed as I went in and squeezed them harder when the doctor closed the door behind him.

CHAPTER 2

SILENCE

The doctors' mint green scrubs showed the maroon splatter from the surgery. I assumed it was from Holly and tried to focus on the fact that she was in recovery. There were three surgeons in all. It was surreal because I was expecting only one. I found myself questioning whether or not she was actually in recovery and if she had pulled through at all. Just exactly how critical was she?

A tall, thin woman took off her glasses and motioned for me to sit at the small table. I pulled the chair out and sat. Then the two male doctors removed their masks and joined me. They weren't smiling.

"Mrs. Williams," one of them said.

"How bad is it?"

The woman sat forward and leaned on the table, cradling her glasses. "We don't expect a full recovery."

My heart was in my throat. "What do you mean?" I asked.

"Your sister had extensive injuries, most of which need to heal on their own, but she had a collapsed lung. When you see her, she will have a chest tube to drain the blood from internal bleeding. She has three broken ribs, a fractured pelvis," she took a breath, "and her spinal cord was severely injured."

"But she's going to live, right?"

One of the male doctors nodded, "We expect her to, she'll be in Critical Intensive Care for a night or two, after that we'll see. But she may never walk again. She's going to need long-term physical therapy, and possibly occupational as well. We'll know better when she's awake and speaking. She has a concussion that we determined needed full sedation."

The other male doctor chimed in. "She's going to have to go to a rehabilitation center and you should expect her to be there a while. Long-term may turn into residency depending on how she recovers. We know more when she is awake, and we can see how her brain is functioning. But for now, expect her to be in a wheelchair."

I was trying to grasp as much medical terminology that I could so that I could communicate it to the rest of our family. "Thank you." What more could I say? They saved her life. They weren't at the accident site, so they couldn't give me any details on the incident. They couldn't tell me who was at fault, and they couldn't explain anything other than a bleak future. But I trusted God to follow through with his plan and breathed into my shaking hands, poised in prayer as quiet tears filled my eyes. "Thank you."

The doctors stood together, and each shook my hand. "I wish we could say more, but right now it's a waiting game for us all."

"I understand," I said. "Can I see her?"

They glanced at each other, then the female doctor said, "She's still pretty out of it. Go get yourself some dinner, a cup of coffee, and take your time. When you come back, she should be ready. Right now, they're still taking care of her postoperative needs. The nurse will text you when it's okay to see her. Why don't you give me your number so I can make sure they have the correct one?"

"Okay," I gave her my number.

"Have a good night, Mrs. Williams."

I nodded, feeling a mass of fresh tears welling up and knew that they would spill once they left the room. They closed the door behind them, and I swallowed. The tears came in streams. I wasn't sure if I was relieved that she was going to live or if I was feeling her pain just from knowing the injuries. Or was I fearing what kind of life she was going to have once the sedation wore off?

I don't really know what I was expecting to hear. I knew she was critical. That was not good. I supposed a few broken ribs were a normal sort of issue, but the lung had me worried. Internal bleeding and a chest tube? How long would that continue? It seemed they were as clueless as I was at that point. The pelvis didn't sound so bad. I met people on my job as a pharmaceutical rep who had hip replacements, cracked pelvises, and even a lung transplant. So, what we were looking at for severity had to be brain trauma and spinal injury. I should have asked more questions.

I dabbed my face with the tissue and stuffed it in my purse. When I left the little room, I noticed the father and daughter were gone. I hoped they were visiting their loved one and that she would have a full recovery. In fact, I closed my eyes and said a little prayer for them before I walked to the elevators.

The cafeteria was closed, so I left the hospital to grab a bite of something along the strip. I wasn't even sure what was around. The hospital was dark, crowded, and downtown. Holly was life-flighted here because the hospital often receives trauma patients. It wasn't like the rural hospitals that I was used to. My stomach was in knots from the news, and now a new tension thanks to the doctors, and then hunger. It was nauseating. I hoisted my purse over my shoulder and walked out of the hospital with my chin up because that's how I always got through the unknowns. It was how I kept from crying and stayed focus on where I was going. I walked that way on purpose when my fears were high. And right then, they were higher than my hope.

On the street, the softly glowing streetlights kept the dark at bay. There were just as many people bustling by

as there was when I arrived. I scanned the buildings for a sign that offered food because my palette didn't care. I just needed something to fill the void, and if they had coffee, it would be a plus.

I spotted a sign for a family pizzeria and restaurant. It was open for another hour. I pulled the door handle and walked in. I felt my senses reawakening with the aroma of garlic and basil. The bells chimed behind me when the door swung closed. An older woman behind the counter grabbed a menu and a set of silverware wrapped in plastic and hurried to greet me. I managed to scan the prepared pizzas in the display case before she directed me to an open table, so I knew what I wanted.

"Just one?" she asked.

"Yes, please."

She put the wrapped ware and the menu down in front of the chair. I pulled it out and sat. The woman had a small notepad and pen poised while she waited for me to finish getting settled.

"Drink?"

"Do you have coffee?" I asked.

She nodded and left.

I glanced over the menu not really looking at anything in particular. I knew I was not going to be allowed in to see Holly anytime soon, but it didn't stop the urge to leave from the restaurant to run back into the waiting room. The woman returned with an evergreen mug filled to the brim with steaming goodness. She set it on the table, but I snatched it up to sip. I felt the beverage was my anchor to not losing my calm and sipping the scorching liquid fulfilled its purpose. I relaxed into the chair and ordered something I didn't even find on the menu.

"A veggie personal sized pizza with alfredo sauce on the side."

She looked at me, "I'll bring it to you right away." She squeezed my wrist and nodded. "Your loved one is in God's hands. It is the best place for any of us to be. "

I stared at her long, slender fingers. The nails were short, but filed. Her hands were clean, strong, and riddled with raised veins that were visible through thinned skin. I placed my other hand on hers.

"Thank you."

I couldn't explain it, but the feeling she gave me in that moment caused goosebumps to cover my body. I felt her spirit connect with mine. I believe she felt my worry. Her words were simple, ones I knew well. Words I believed deep in my heart, but still I feared the outcome. Somehow, being reminded eased the tension in my chest. My stomach lurched, reminding me I hadn't eaten a real meal the entire day. A few snacks, but that was all.

I held my phone, triple checking my text messages. Yes, I was told that they would call when she was ready for me to see her, but I didn't trust the system. *What if they got my number wrong?* But I gave it to more than

one person. They were professionals who did this every day. I had to have trust. I had to believe in the people put in her path. She was going to live. So, what caused my fear? The fact that she may never walk, that my spicy sister may be a paraplegic, was not the ideal scenario, but it was most definitely better than other circumstances.

Holly and I were never super close. Not like Becky and me. For some reason, she felt the need to let life handle her. From getting pregnant as a teen to quitting high school. My parents never set up boundaries for my siblings and me as children. My sisters were almost always in a relationship with boys, even as teenagers. The day Holly came home to tell Mom and Dad was one of the loudest in the house. I really don't know if it was the fact that she was pregnant or the fact that the father of the child had many of the same characteristics of my father—both under-employed and under the influence.

She stepped through the door that day, her eyes glazed over with tears. "Jen, can you get Mom?"

I pressed her to tell me what was going on. She was visibly upset, but there was fear behind the tears. Without another question, I ran to the back of the trailer and woke my mother. "Mom, Holly wants to talk to you. I think it's important," I whispered, careful not to wake my father.

"What?" she said, pulling herself out of the bed and straightening her T-shirt and shorts. "Where is she?"

"In the living room."

I turned to exit, with my mother closing the bedroom door behind her. We all knew the rage-filled outbursts my father exhibited for no reason, and they were more frequent and violent, especially when he was hungover. Holly was sitting on the couch, clutching a handmade pillow.

"Mom, I'm pregnant," Holly said when we entered the room.

"What did you just say?" she yelled. "Pregnant?"

My sister stared at the shag carpet on the floor. She was silent.

"What, nothing to say for yourself?" my mother demanded, her voice getting louder and higher in pitch. "Is the father who I think it is?" Her boyfriend of choice was known to belittle all females and proudly boasted he had several children from other young women.

I can only assume that we roused my father from his sleep when my mother left the room. The shouting must have piqued his curiosity and intervention. He barreled down the hall and slammed his hand on the counter, spilling papers and a plastic plate to the floor.

I could see by his flushed face he was not in control. "Dad, don't do it," I said.

"Shut up," he slurred. I guessed the alcohol still impaired him from the previous late night. "Pregnant by who? When?" Then he turned on my mother, shouting at her she was to blame.

Holly's tears streamed down her cheeks, and she stared at the floor, not answering.

"Dad, please," I said, just wanting him to stop.

"I told you before to shut up. Are you next? Tell me, Holly, are you planning on raising this child or expecting us to do it?" He was out of control, calling her every name in the book that came to his unloving, disgusting mind. He even berated my mother for giving birth to us, and me, because I was there.

The more he ranted, the louder he became. The irony of my father's madness was that everything he was angry about occurred in his life. He had two children that he didn't associate with before he married my mom—half-siblings who, to this day, I have never met. His life spiraled out of control and he succumbed to the calling of drugs and alcohol. Keeping a steady job and providing for your family—well, that was optional in his eyes.

Holly covered her ears and rocked in her seat on the worn cushion.

No matter what he said, and even after my mother lured him outside to continue his tirade, Holly said nothing. I could feel the effect of my father's anger, even without his presence.

I sat beside her, not touching because she wasn't a hugger, but I didn't want to leave her alone to fight this battle. And now, sitting in this pizzeria, I was determined to stay by her side once again. But this time it wasn't because of a battle with my father, but one with her own mind that I knew would be coming. Change is constant, and I knew that Holly's life had forever changed.

When the pizza came, I rushed through eating it, drizzling the alfredo sauce over the top and taking sips of now tepid coffee to cool the piping hot melted cheese and sauces. I still scalded my mouth, but memories of Holly that day so many years ago reminded me that silence is worth a thousand words, and I wanted to be at her side to understand her silence once again.

I finished the whole pizza, and a refilled coffee before leaving cash on the table with a hundred percent tip. I didn't have time to collect change, and the sweet, elderly woman offered me comfort and understanding. It was the least I could do.

* * *

Once I was back in the waiting room, it took an additional twenty minutes before I received a text. She was in post-op. I could see her. I collected myself and strode toward the double doors and paused before pressing the button on the wall.

You can do this, Jenna, I told myself.

I pushed and the doors swung open. When I stepped through, a nurse in pink scrubs approached me.

"Ms. Williams? I understand you are Holly's sister and authorized to make decisions on her behalf."

"Yes," I said.

"When you see her, she's not going to look like you remember. There will be IV lines and she's on high flow oxygen therapy. She's awake, but not enough to talk. Did the doctors discuss her condition with you?"

I nodded and followed her to a curtained room in the back. "We're preparing a room in the Intensive Care Unit. When she's medically ready to leave the hospital, she'll most likely be transferred to a rehabilitation facility. The social worker will be in contact with you to discuss those details."

"Thank you."

The nurse stepped aside, letting me go behind the curtain. She took her spot at the computer cart outside of the room. I glanced back at her as a form of lifeline. If I felt like crying, I knew she was there. I would suck it up for my sister. Knowing that the feelings I was experiencing were inside me—I scurried to organize them.

I walked with measured steps to her bedside and scanned the scene before me. The doctor wrapped her head in white gauze. Crumbled glass and matted, bloody hair peeked through the gauze. They also tucked an oxygen tube into her nostrils and inserted a chest catheter just beneath her collarbone. Three bags of IV fluid ran through a line in the back of her hand and I spotted the tracheostomy tube in her throat under. One arm was in a sling and it seemed her legs lay motionless under the sheet. She was lying flat on her back, and a stiff pink neck brace was under her neck, keeping her head immobile.

"Hey, Hol," I said in a soft, cheerful voice.

Her eyes fluttered but didn't open.

"You look," I paused. *Does she even know what happened?* "How do you feel?"

A breathy sigh escaped her lips. I took it as a response. "It can only get better from here. We've been through hell together before."

I ran my finger over the back of the hand extending from the sling, unable to avoid the tears. I didn't try to stop them. I welcomed them because crying was something I could do. Otherwise, I was useless. There was nothing I could do but wait. I studied the color of her face and glanced down to see a bag hanging on the side of the bed fill with trickling blood. *The chest tube. Right, internal bleeding.*

The nurse brought a chair so I could sit and offered me a ginger ale. "It looks worse than it is." She pointed at the monitor that was mounted on the wall. "Her blood pressure is stable. Her rhythm is steady. Her oxygen is holding at 97, and the tube ensures it stays that way. It's going to take time, Ms. Williams." She left me there,

stroking my sister's hand. Holly being alive was nothing short of a miracle.

I placed the ginger ale on the service table and laid my head down beside her. Unsure of her consciousness, I wept. I wanted answers. My mind filtered through all that had happened. I wanted to know how the accident happened, how she felt and what she remembered. The streams of salty tears turned into sobs. I gripped the blanket and let myself go for the first time since the call. Little did I know it wouldn't be the last.

CHAPTER 3

BREAK THROUGH

Holly was in her room at the rehabilitation center. Although the center's decor hadn't been updated in years, it was known to be the best around. She was finally in a single room with her bed facing the large window. The nurse opened the shades, but there was no sunshine. The gray skies grew darker by the second. A storm was rolling in from the southwest. Coupled with the parking lot view, it was a dark scene, but I didn't care. I enjoyed the rain.

My mind drifted. When Holly and I were kids, we'd run outside into the rain with a bar of soap. We would laugh and point our faces up to the sky to catch raindrops on our tongues. But too much rain turned to storms. Living in shambles near the Indiana bayou meant flooding and raging waters. Wind brought down trees and tornadoes occurred more than a handful of times in my youth. Lightning seemed to hit right outside my window.

I hated storms.

The wind rocked the mobile home and beads of water sounded like metal hitting the roof. Leaks in the ceiling seams created the need for us to makeshift a bandage to prevent or control water. There was one particular leak in the bathroom where water always streamed down the wall. The ceiling was rotted and yellow. After the rains, mold grew in the spot leaving a musty smell. The damp bayou created the perfect breeding ground for all sorts of things.

The area we lived in was part of Cypress Bayou, ripe with wildlife and large cypress trees. The Cache River was home to the famed Tupelo trees and the bald cypress. There were herons, foxes, and water moccasins. Badgers, martens, and coyotes were often seen or heard. Wild bobcats called the grounds home along with a number of bloodsucking insects. We loved swimming in the river when it was calm, but the flood waters always caused massive destruction. We had a yellow canoe and a rowboat that we used to traverse the waters when it was safe. The world was our oyster, or at least that was the way I remembered it.

Holly stirred in her bed, bringing me back to the moment. I watched the storm clouds descending on the distant hills. It was a matter of moments before it reached the parking lot. Holly hadn't started her physical therapy for the day, and the occupational therapist was called off for a family emergency. Since her admittance to the facility, Holly developed a loathing for the place and the people. She'd rotated through several shared rooms until a single room

was available. The social worker said it was common for people who experience a grave trauma to feel angry for a while.

But I knew my sister. This was more than anger and adjustment. She struggled with depression throughout her life, and now I felt like she was battling her value even more while coping with her new limitations. I wished I could get Holly to understand that she was so much more than just her physical body. Her soul was thirsting to direct her; however, this wasn't the time to try to convince her. The rain beating on the window ledge didn't moisten her skin. She couldn't splash in the puddles or gasp from a passing car soaking the bottom of her trousers. She would never again run through the downpour, hoping to escape waterlogged clothes.

Her legs wouldn't work; couldn't work.

When they first brought her to the facility, I was there, ready to hold her hand. She blinked away tears and closed her eyes. Three weeks into rehab, and she was still unable to lift her feet or move her legs.

"Hey, Holl," I said, wanting to rouse her from her lethargy.

"Hmm?" she mumbled.

"I brought you something. I think you'll like it." I hummed. "What's your favorite color?"

Her chest compressed in a quick, purposeful fashion. That was her way of sighing at me, exasperated. I reminded myself that emotions were good. But her willingness to try had waned. I needed her to get her vivacious spirit back. She was a spitfire woman with spirit—always saying what she pleased. Whether or not we agreed, she had an inner fire that pushed her, motivated her. I wanted to tap into that old flame—to find the burning ember to rekindle what was left.

The day before, my husband Bryce and I went to the mall searching for something that would resonate with her. I held teddy bear carcasses that needed someone to love, wooden roses, sweet smelling lotions, and glitter lamps. Each item represented something my sister enjoyed, but had no purpose for where she was. They would all sit collecting dust. It was pointless. I was in search for something that would give light to her.

As I scanned the store front displays, a shoe store caught my attention. "Hey, Bryce," I said, bumping his elbow and pointing to the wall of sneakers.

"She can't use them; it will just make her sink deeper into an already unbearable depression. She doesn't need a reminder of what she will never be able to do again." He held my hand, rubbing the back with his thumb. "I know you want to help Holly, Jen. But you need to think about who she is and what would appeal to that new person."

I disagreed. I knew new shoes would spark a dose of the willpower that Holly needed. An old memory popped into my head. I was an elementary student and

I remember being selected to leave class. We ventured to the school parking lot where an unidentified shoe bus was parked. The shoe bus offered a wide selection of shoes for underprivileged kids. We were properly fitted and left with a pair of shoes. The act of kindness offered from the group running the shoe bus is something I carry with me today. Having new shoes that fit correctly was a tremendous confidence builder.

I smiled at Bryce, pulled away, and made a dash for the women's athletic shoes. There, like a beacon on a clear night, was a pair of hot pink track shoes. The salesperson saw me coming and headed in my direction. "They are a statement, aren't they?" she enthused.

"Do they come in size nine?" I asked.

She took off toward a doorway leading to the storeroom and called over her shoulder. "Let me check. I think I may have them in the back." The woman disappeared while I waited by the cash register, card in hand.

Bryce leaned on the counter; his big, brown eyes full of concern. "Jen, it's a mistake. I'm telling you."

"I know my sister, Bryce. If anything is going to motivate her, it will be the realization that she *can't* do something. Throughout her whole life, every time she was told she couldn't do something, it made her defiant. She loves pink, and she hasn't had a new pair of sneakers like this in a long time. If she sees these on her feet . . ." the saleswoman emerged carrying a box.

"You're in luck. Would you like to try them on?"

"Oh, they're a gift," I said, handing her my gold card. I turned to my husband. "I'm telling you; she's going to love them."

"I hope you're right, babe. I hope you're right." He shook his head when I added neon socks and laces to the order.

Now that I was standing in Holly's room holding the plastic shopping bag with the bright pink sneakers, I felt the pang of apprehension in my gut. I wanted her to love them. To slide her feet into the shoes, swing her feet over the edge of the bed, and take her first steps. I knew it wouldn't happen; couldn't happen. But I wasn't about to let it bring me down. I made my way around the bed so that I was in front of her.

"I brought a present for you," I said.

She blinked and pursed her lips.

"I know you can speak. Come on, now. Aren't you the least bit curious?"

"Not really," she said.

"Good, you're speaking to me. It's working." I pulled the bag out from behind my back. "Want me to open it for you?"

"Sure" she answered.

"Because there's no fun in looking at a white plastic bag."

She closed her eyes again. "Alright, let's go."

"Great!" I sat on the side of her bed and pulled out the shoe-box, letting the bag slide to the floor.

Holly shook her head. "Are you serious? Shoes. It'll be a while before I can use those—if ever." Blood rushed to her cheeks and her entire face flushed. "What were you thinking, Jenna? I can't walk. I'll never be able to walk. Take them back."

"Nope. You were told you can't. That is not the same as working toward achieving an outcome. You can't give up." I opened the lid on the box and handed it to her.

She moved the tissue paper aside and ran her hand over the pink fabric. "They are really pretty."

"Aren't they? No one ever said you can't wear shoes. You love pink, and these are as pink as pink gets. Let me put them on you."

She fumbled with the paper and covered the sneakers. "Not right now."

"I'm not taking them home, Hol. You can wear them for therapy. I'll be here every day, and I want to see you wearing them. I know you like them, and they'll be a lot more comfortable and supportive than house slippers. You need this." It was the way I was, and the way I would always be. Supportive and optimistic.

My mind flashed with another memory. They weren't

always rough times in our younger years. There were also positives I recalled from my childhood. Some of them being my immense imagination, bigger than anyone could believe. I'd dream crazy big dreams, because there were only two choices when it came down to what mattered. Either you think super small or super big. I chose super big. I always felt like there was something more in store for me outside of our usual family experience.

I took the shoe box from Holly's hands and put it in her dresser drawer. "When the physical therapist comes tomorrow, I will present them to you again." I was determined to practice this exercise with wit.

* * *

The next day, I arrived back at the center, ready to face Holly's depression head on. She was going to meet the therapist with her new sneakers and learn that her life wasn't over. It was changed, and yes, it sucked. It was going to be a long haul before any progress was made, but she had a team in her corner.

My mother stayed alongside Holly as well much of the time. She captured several pictures along the journey. And I started to journal her recovery on a medical communication site that co-workers and family could follow and leave encouraging comments for me to share with Holly.

When I walked into the room, the nurse propped up

in bed with her breakfast tray in front of her. She hadn't eaten. "Oh, man. What is that?" I asked, joking like we always did.

"Normal crap."

"Oh, like mom's *gar-bage?*" I was referring to what our mother always called 'the stuff I gathered together to make dinner.' She said it with a French accent to make it sound fancy and to make us laugh. In all honesty, most of her dishes were amazing. I am in awe of how she did it.

Holly rolled her eyes. Working in the restaurants all of her life, our mother taught us how presentation of the food made the meal taste better than it actually was. The food in front of Holly offered no mouthwatering presentation.

I moved closer to the bed so I could brush the hair from her eyes and take in the stuff they were trying to feed her. "It doesn't look too bad. A slice of bread, scrambled eggs, and peanut butter. A yogurt and an apple for later."

"They can take it," she said flatly.

"You have to eat something, Holly. You need your strength. The protein will help with the healing." I went to the dresser and pulled out the shoe-box. "Ready to try them on?"

"Actually, Jen. No." She pushed the food tray away on the rolling stand and hoisted herself higher in her bed. "I don't need a pair of sneakers. I'm not going to walk. And I really don't need your bubbling personality to come in here every single day, reminding me of how my life didn't turn out. You keep reminding me of all the things that I need to do. I get it—life worked out for you— college, marriage, kids. I just want to *be*. I can't even use the bathroom by myself, let alone walk!"

"Holly, don't say that." I reminded myself this was just part of the psychological healing process and her emotions were valid. I should be celebrating the fact that she was engaging. "I'm glad you're sharing how you feel with me."

"You can go, Jenna. Go spend your time with your family. Mom is here with me. We will figure this out." Tears leaked from the corners of her eyes.

"No. You can say what you want about me, but keep in mind you're my family. Growing up, I struggled too. I felt alone. I was always the odd man out. I had no choice but to learn to embrace my fears. I said it when we were little and it's true today; the way we lived wasn't right. We deserved better. We all made sacrifices, Holly."

"Just go, Jen. I'm tired." Holly turned away and didn't speak for the ten minutes it took for me to get the gumption to leave. I left the pink sneakers on her dresser and paused in the doorway.

"I love you, sis."

I squinted from the sun's reflection on the cars as I emerged from the rehab facility. Holly's reprimand and depression hurt. I expected it to be bad, but I didn't think

she would lash out at me or the life I created for myself, and most importantly, my family. She had no idea the hell I went through in the hours after that call. I had to run from the house, jump in my car and go. I know my brave face faltered at times while I tried to remain optimistic about her condition. In was intent on returning after she had time to decompress.

CHAPTER 4

GROUNDING

Holly's road to healing offered a lot of time to reflect. It is so surreal to think about that fateful day that changed our lives forever. I still can hear my mom's words from her telephone call making me aware of Holly's accident. I remember immediately calling the hospital for details all the while mentally game-planning how I could orchestrate my children without causing them fear.

The nurse said it would be a while, so I hustled my large SUV to school pick up and waited for my two youngest and two teens to emerge. I filled what looked like an amazing designer bag from the outside with used tissues. This fancy bag was used and abused for all aspects of my life. Luckily it was a gift for myself. While the gift was a celebration of my triumph over Hell, my utilization of the bag would be a designer's nightmare seeing it full of crayons, ChapStick and business essentials. I looked in the visor mirror as I dabbed a blot of mascara under my eye. My auburn hair and faded freckles offset the white business suit always made me feel put together.

The suit was mere mommy-wear. It felt good. Life felt good, except my heart hurt for Holly.

The school was a small Catholic school nestled in Merion County, located in central Indiana. The school grounds were alive with smiling faces rushing to meet their parents, the joyous ending to a busy day. It was the best in the region, and I was proud to have my children attend the single-story, brick-sided school and become part of their growing history—a history that would not leave them with unsheddable baggage like I carried.

A father was busy buckling in a squirming toddler, also in a blue uniform consisting of navy shorts and sky-blue shirt. The mother stood by the passenger rear door, scowling as she read a neon orange handout. I smiled because it was the second child who captured my attention. He tossed his backpack in the open trunk and crossed his arms, waiting. He was a little man with a mop of dark brown hair like his dad. He climbed into the Lincoln Navigator with expertise when his mother opened the door. She waited for him to buckle in, then returned to the front seat, folding the paper and tucking it in the sun visor.

My son, Zach, ran from his teacher toward me followed by his sister Hope. Zach's short blonde hair bounced with each footfall. I adored my children. Even after a full day at school, their faces beamed with joy. They are my miracle, a gift from God. I opened the back door, and

Zach climbed into his booster seat, pulling his seatbelt across. Hope shuffled through her homework folder.

"Hi, stranger," I teased, taking the time to kiss the top of his head. I tousled his hair with a quick glance at the roots, a habit I'd never outgrow. He watched me from the corner of his eye.

"You know me, Mommy."

"Ah, but do you know me?"

He giggled.

I leaned in and pressed my forehead to his. "I love you. You know that, right?"

"I love you too," he said.

The teacher waved to me as she went back inside the building. I closed the door waiting for my older two. Ben was thirteen and Meghan was fourteen. I knew better than to make a fuss when they came out, so I slid into the driver's seat, stepping on a goldfish cracker, smearing it into the beige carpet. I scuffed the crumbs aside with the toe of my driving shoe. It didn't bother me because I liked to live in and utilize nice things. I didn't mind the crumbs; it was a reminder of how I was still grounded by motherhood and the joys of simplicity. I earned my wealth with willpower and everything that made me who I was. The last thing I was going to do was pretend to be something I wasn't. A crunched cracker could be vacuumed. Gratitude and peace embraced my soul at school pickup—even on the roughest days.

I glanced at the mother in the car parked beside me. She seemed overwhelmed and scattered. I knew that feeling. I remember feeling overwhelmed in all things new, especially joining the Catholic community, let alone the school community—somewhat unworthy, if you will. I wasn't raised anything like how my children were being raised. In the early days of my journey, I questioned if I deserved this opportunity. I felt as though there was a certain style and lifestyle that I had to mirror. Eventually I decided simply to be present, and most important, just be me.

When the woman looked in my direction, I smiled and waved.

My whole purpose was to enjoy life and that meant crunched crackers, spilled drinks, and dirty tissues in my everyday bag. It filled me with gratitude for the things I had and for the opportunity to have them as I have experienced the other side of the coin—the side where designer clothes and fun foods were a dream. Though it was in my past, the acknowledgement kept me grateful and learning. Judging the outside vessel of another individual wasn't how I did things. I would not look down on any parent who wanted the best for their children or for the exhausted parents who ran around in circles and rescheduled appointment after appointment because they cared. I have learned that knowing someone's true intention is the most important thing to know about

them. We are all clay being molded along this journey of life.

I pulled a pack of fruit snacks from the console, ripped the top off, and handed them back to Zach. "How was your day?" I asked.

He took the package, slid one into his mouth and mumbled, "It was good. We had to tell the teacher what your name was, and Dad's and where you work. I drew a picture."

"Oh," I said. "What did you say?"

"I said that my mom's name is Jen and my dad's name is Bryce and I have a brother and two sisters, and we have a farm and a hundred cows." He smiled at me, swinging his feet. "I drew a picture of our calves with their mamas."

"Hey, mom. Can we have one?" Ben knocked on the driver's side window before opening the back door.

I jumped, spilling my purse on the front seat Meghan was sliding into. "You scared me. Don't do that."

Meghan helped gather the contents of my purse and stuffed it all back inside. "Well, maybe you should be more aware of what's around you. Isn't that what you tell us? Do you have any more snacks?"

I frowned at her, then laughed. The woman behind me must have thought I was nuts, but I didn't care. I took out three packs and handed my older two theirs, keeping the third for myself. It was tiny moments like this I cherished. They knew I would be there, and that I had their needs covered. I loved that my children felt open to share their days and desires with me.

I had made a name for myself, Jenna Williams. I'd come a long way, but not far enough. Because the smile I gave my precious children was fake. I wanted to feel the real joy, but I had to settle for the kind that lived behind the resentment that festered just under the surface. Tears wet my lashes, but I blinked them away, hoping to keep the kids from seeing how I truly felt, though they would know once I dropped them off at home with their father.

Home meant our farmhouse sitting on ten acres with ten chickens, two 4H goats and a slew of cattle, with enough room to safely love our family. It was heaven to us because Bryce and I personally designed and general contracted the whole project. But today, this one single call tore my heart out. It was reminiscent of when I was not much older than Ben and the life-altering phone call came about my dad.

The kids munched on their snacks. Zach watched the landscape roll by and my other kids prepped homework for the next day. My mind dredged up memories of my past. The real struggle started when I was five, or at least that's as far back as I remember.

I could visualize my childhood home, clear as day. We had an enormous mulberry tree out front. The trunk was thick and split in two, opening into an enormous

umbrella of dark green leaves. In spring, the tiny white flower blossoms would cover the slender limbs. The fragrance was sweet and welcoming. Once the flowers turned to white berries, we watched and waited for them to turn into the long red and black fruits we loved. My sisters Holly, Becky, my brother Mark, and I would climb to the top with five-gallon ice cream buckets to collect the berries.

When the buckets were full, we'd come down with purple stained feet and fingers. The road we lived on was unpaved, and the smell of mosquito spray being dispersed by county trucks stained the air. It was a tar and pea gravel sort of road that sprouted tar bubbles in the hot sun. We could hear the buzz of the power lines overhead when we walked along the country roads. The roads were lined with thick bushes and trees with the prettiest greens. I loved leaning out of the car window when riding down our road, reaching to collect the greenest ones.

Our home was less than modest. We lived on a road that formed a 'T' with our house in the middle. We even had a concrete drain under the road that I adventured through to get to the other side. Becky and I would spend several hours playing pretend in the concrete drain. It was often coated in spider webs and made the coolest sounds when cars drove over the roadway above it. There were times that we didn't have running water or regular heat. As a backup, we had a kerosene heater that would leave soot on the ceiling and everything else, including our lungs and our noses. Having a family our size meant lots of laundromat visits or quick handwashing clothes when we couldn't get out. We tried our best to look like we lived normally, but I believe others could tell we didn't. There were times my mother would either buy or fill water jugs for washing and drinking. We became avid campers, supposedly great family time, but in reality, a time for having reliable utilities.

The bugs in the house were more comfortable than I was until the lights flashed on and they would scatter. They would run into the crevices and through the black grime between the refrigerator and stove. They hovered in the drawers and lived off the compressed wood in the flooring and walls. This living environment became our default home. There were phases when we moved around from rentals to a rent-to-own home my mom was going to buy. Each move meant changing schools, changing friends and changing family dynamics. When things didn't work out, we always defaulted to moving back to the bayou. I guess it was the bottom of the barrel.

Growing up as the freckle-face, redhead of the family, I was so different from the rest. They had brown hair and brown eyes, all of them. I guess that's why the school nurse always found the lice on me and then continued to my brother and sisters. Of course, I couldn't say which

was worse, sitting in the office waiting for someone to pick up the phone, or getting picked up to come home to an angry, drunk father who on another "break" from work yet another time.

Of course, I couldn't blame my mother for not getting the calls. Half the time our service was cut off for nonpayment. Ironically, it still worked from the phone pole. Crazy that we literally found a way around a disconnected phone line. When the phone service was shut off, it was still available from the phone pole. These were the kind of backup plans I was taught as a child. A roadblock was never the end of the road. There was always a way around it.

So, yeah. Even at five, I was not okay with our lifestyle, and I was very vocal about how not okay it was and how it was far from normal. Impressive as that may seem to the unknowing bystander, I had unrealistic circumstances unfold because of my strong sense of spirit. In truth, I felt a presence of a spirit, mostly when I slept. And I never felt alone. As a child. I would close my eyes and feel the spirit over the top left side of my head. I remember the presence feeling so big that I was too intimidated to look at it directly, but it was so comforting to know it was there. I always felt a calling for something bigger than I could visually see. My parents laughed at me when I was in kindergarten. On Sundays, I would catch a bus alone to attend service at a Baptist church. It gave me a sense of belonging and peace. I gradually became aware that the warm presence that I felt was guiding me, keeping me safe and was always with me—it was my spirit.

And now, as a forty-year-old mother, I was dropping my kids off at our bountiful home because of a needless accident. The police called my mother to let her know that my sister Holly had been in a head-on collision and was life-lined to a hospital near me. The other driver in a pickup truck swerved over the double yellow line into oncoming traffic. Holly was hit from the front by him, and rear-ended by another pickup. Her Kia Forte was no match for two trucks. She was in surgery when I called the hospital, so I gathered the kids and let them see me, because I had the feeling that it was going to be a long night. My brother couldn't be reached, and Becky was out of town.

I pulled into the garage, bringing me back to the moment. Bryce was waiting for the kids with the egg basket in his hands. I wished I could join them.

"I have to go check on Aunt Holly and won't be home until late. See you later. I love you." I was glad they didn't understand the severity of the situation, but my amazing husband Bryce did. The kids gave me a kiss and dashed into the house to change into their work clothes.

"You sure you want to go to the hospital in that?" he asked, eyeing the white pantsuit.

"Right," I said. "I'll go change."

I did just that and was back in the car before ten minutes passed. It riddled me with guilt over leaving my sister at the hospital for the hour it took after learning of the accident and the surgery to pick up the kids. My food intake consisted of fruit snacks and stale black coffee leftover from my morning sales meeting. After changing into a comfortable pair of blue jeans and an oversized sweatshirt, I hopped in the car. I figured I would grab a fresh coffee in the hospital cafeteria once I knew she was stable.

Hearing the word 'critical' come from any medical professional's mouth is nauseating. It stole my appetite when I thought about it. That day, I headed back to the hospital in hopes of a positive outcome.

Today I was entering the rehabilitation center with a double order of Starbucks. It was a new day; the perfect time for a good cup of coffee to share with my sister.

CHAPTER 5

TIME

They say time stands still for no one. It was clear that it didn't for me or Bryce, my kids, or Holly. Life was going to do whatever it planned to do, no matter what anyone said or did. I walked into Holly's room and put her coffee on the nightstand.

She was asleep.

I sat in the chair tucked in the corner and contemplated waking her. The truth was, I could not fault her for feeling down about her physical condition. I loved my own vitality. But her depression stemmed from more than that. The truth sucked. I was busy picking up my kids from school, attending meetings, and orchestrating marketing for my job.

Why wouldn't she be angry with me? I reasoned.

She lost a lot, but she still had her children. Holly was a single mother. Her children were pretty much self-sufficient, since they were all adults. Big life changes were ahead of her.

I sipped my coffee—black with sugar.

"Wow," I said. I watched her blanket move slightly. She wasn't sleeping. She was faking it. "Funny how things come to mind at the oddest moments. Like Mom." I sipped again. "She loved plants. Especially marigolds, yellow roses, blouses, and black coffee with sugar." I looked inside the sippy hole in the lid. "Guess some things get passed down without us realizing."

"She tried. That's what mattered," Holly said.

I smiled. Strange, I was actually just talking. It wasn't an attempt for her to join me, but it made my heart warm. "Being a mom is worth its weight in gold. I can't imagine having to raise the kids the way she raised us."

Holly opened her eyes. "Do you remember her uniforms?"

"I do. Mom always worked in the restaurant industry."

"Yeah," she said, pulling herself up, eyeing the paper cup of coffee. "Mostly the late shift unless she was covering for someone else."

I remembered those days. She came home reeking of smoke from the restaurant. Her uniform was stiff from grease and nicotine. When I was young, I didn't realize how often she went to work with black eyes and bruises. My mom became a natural at making up excuses or stories to avoid reality. As kids, we too learned to fib to teachers when they asked about our situation at home. I always prayed for God to take me from there. I felt the adults around me should have done more to find a way to give me a better life. I asked why I had to go through these tests. I was faithful. I now know that these

childhood tests taught me skills needed to overcome obstacles along my journey.

Becky and I stayed away from my father when he was on a rampage until he was out cold snoring, and we were sure he was passed out. Then we would grab whatever we could and go to our room. My brother was off getting high with his friends from the time he was in his early teens. He and Holly would venture in and out of the house as they deemed fit. Frequently, the school would reach out to my mother noting an abundance of absences, but they never investigated.

Even when it was good, it was bad. I remember curling up to hang out with my father in the living room. He would often sit in the single chair with an end table next to him where he placed his dented can of beer. I loved watching NBA games on Friday nights with him, especially the Chicago Bulls. He'd holler at the TV and test me on the players backgrounds and stories until he passed out. I'd fall asleep on the couch and somehow always woke up to the Monkees Show the next morning.

He managed to keep the same job at the industrial company even though he missed so many days and would quit time after time. Sometimes he'd come home from work during the week and blast REO Speedwagon or Journey on the record player and turn it up so loud the speakers vibrated. He loved his records. He'd grab a beer and sing along. We even danced to the music. As a kid it meant a lot. I had to take what I could get.

It broke my heart to imagine doing that, or Bryce doing that, to our kids.

Amazing how a good cup of coffee turned to a rabbit hole of past reflections of our living Hell. I put my cup on the window ledge and rubbed my palms on my pants. "You know, all of your kids are rooting for you to get back home."

"Jesus, if I wear the damn sneakers will you promise to go away?" Holly asked.

"No, but I will promise to be here for you no matter how many times you treat me like dirt. There's nothing you can dish that's as bad as Dad's crap," I said.

"Why are you doing this?"

"Because you're my sister. I know we aren't close, but we're blood. I love you." I picked up the coffee and chugged it. "Why are you fighting this?"

"I'm accepting it, Jenna. You're the one who's living in some lala land. I don't want to waste my time doing exercises that hurt, leave me exhausted and in the end aren't going to do anything for me. I'm paralyzed." She turned to look at the wall, blinking away tears. "I should have died. It would have been better for everyone. Just move on. This is dragging it out."

"I know you don't want to hear it, but you have to

have faith. Faith in yourself, if nothing else. Come on. What have you got to lose?"

* * *

Over the next six weeks, Bryce and I went to the rehab center to work with Holly. She learned how to use a wheelchair and worked on supporting her own weight on her legs with the help of a walker. Each day, she grew stronger. The muscle atrophy started to reverse. If we had normal jobs, it would have been an issue, but we were self-employed. Perhaps it was luck or part of a divine plan. She was trying, but her attitude about work differed from mine.

I started working as soon as I could at the age of fourteen. Like my mother, I focused on restaurants mostly hosting or cashiering. Restaurants offered a flexible schedule for school even though they only paid minimum wage. I loved the ability to speak with so many people. I was a people pleaser to both my managers and the customers. Work somehow became an outlet and something I could control and grow with, even at such an early age.

My work experience encouraged me to think about business—marketing, making a profit, managing customers and inventory. In school, I joined DECA, a business club, and learned all that there was to know about business, or so I thought. By the time I was a sophomore,

I developed an interest in journalism. Academically, I was a good student and learning came easy to me. I was well behaved and disciplined. The importance of an education was something I understood from the time I could read. It gave me an outlet, an escape from my life. When I didn't have adventures to devour, I picked up encyclopedias. The older the book, the better.

It didn't matter because I wanted to learn. I wanted to learn about everything. Both my parents were always patching together transportation for our family. The thought of diagnosing a problem and fixing it intrigued me, so I signed up for auto mechanics in high school with a friend. We learned the basics of pistons, cylinders, oil, and brakes. I recognized a lot of the verbiage from my parents and the laid-back atmosphere of the students who took that class was great, too.

I joined a work-study program my senior year, allowing me to do my studies half the day at school and conduct business credits by working at Hobby Lobby the rest of the day. I was geared up to start college through Ivy Tech in January of my senior year. Ivy Tech offered a free class, so I seized the opportunity. I became interested in nutrition and fitness plus working out to build strength and endurance. That led me to eating a balanced meal with my own hard-earned money. Nutrition was not something my parents understood or implemented. There was no pairing of carbohydrates to proteins. Five

vegetables a day was impossible when the entire meal consisted of a single can of whatever our mother had in the pantry. I was grateful for my own paychecks and I was accruing knowledge.

All that time spent working fueled a desire to become better. I wanted more out of life than working late night shifts with creepy customers like my mother experienced. I didn't want to become a statistic. As I watched my siblings venture in their own directions outside of education and having children, I wondered what was next for them. I remember questioning if they were living life the way it was 'supposed to be.' I felt wedged between what I knew as normal and what I wanted as abnormal—perspective was everything.

A friend mentioned his girlfriend was attending a prestigious, all-girls Catholic college in the coming fall. He painted this amazing picture of midnight mass, dorm life, the beautiful woods like campus. It all sounded amazing. The overwhelming challenge was the cost to attend. I am not sure if it was my ego or my spirit that sparked a fire for me to attend that particular college, but I was determined.

College was so unnatural to me. I had zero experience on what the traditional college path looked like. The path kept drawing me in, however there were so many obstacles. I mailed the application during a window of waived application fees. I zeroed in on the deadlines to complete the admissions process. Similar to how I was raised, there would be roadblock after roadblock, and I would have to pave a path around each of them. I could not get my mom to fill out financial information, so I had to prove why I should be able to apply as independent. This didn't sound traditional. Nothing about me was traditional—nope, I was an exception—I was independent. I borrowed a book from the public library and wrote for as many grants and scholarships as I could. I had no idea what this really meant, but I saw an opportunity there to gain funding for something I wanted to do, so I did it. The day finally came; a vanilla-linen letter arrived in the mail. The college accepted me! The journey was beginning, and I had no idea how to prepare.

"Hey, Holly," I said.

She grimaced at me. "What?"

"Remember when I got into college, the only one I applied to?"

"What about it?" she asked.

"I had hope. Yeah, I had good grades, but that doesn't mean you get in. I have hope in you too. You've been asked to take part in a clinical trial. Sure, you aren't guaranteed to get the drug and maybe you'll get a placebo, but regardless, there's hope! They're willing to put their faith in you." I motioned to the hallway outside. "The surgeons replaced your hips. You were supposed

to be a quadriplegic, but here you are rolling over and hoisting and pressing buttons on the bed to sit up, and after a short time in the medical world's eyes. What have you got to lose?"

"What if it doesn't work?"

"Then you got a great pair of sneakers and a workout. Whether or not you can walk, you still need to exercise. If it works, then you've made a huge difference in so many lives, people in the future counting on you. There's a panel of medical professionals who believe you're a perfect candidate. Right now, it comes down to you. What do you say? Will you give it a try?"

CHAPTER 6

ONE STEP
BACK

It had been a month since Holly decided to give her therapy sessions her all. The doctors were in awe of her progress, and the therapists became her cheerleaders. I showed up every day and Bryce came with me most of the time. It was easier to schedule meetings than to change the kids' school events, so I went in the late mornings. The journaling of Holly's journey became a therapy of my own for family and friends. I would always share her ups and downs. I loved reading all the warm wishes and prayers shared from family and friends with Holly.

We were happy for many days, though she would experience a loss of sensation in her right leg, which caused her to stumble at times. Those created the hardest moments because it discouraged her. As much as she had us in her corner, rooting for every step, her motivation depleted. But I persevered. My momentum and motivation didn't falter.

If I stumbled, Bryce was there to pull me forward.

That is, until one Saturday in late August. My sister Becky called my cell. I missed it because I was with Holly and the physical therapist. We were discussing the next steps. Holly was moving her legs, bearing weight, and taking small steps. They wanted to send her home with exercises but didn't want to lose the progress she had made.

Since I didn't answer, Becky called Bryce. Normally, he waited for us in Holly's room, but this time, he showed up in the therapist's office. He knocked on the solid wooden door.

"Come in," Roger called. He sat back in his chair, a frown betraying his annoyance at being interrupted. "I don't like to be interrupted when I'm in a conference."

I understood and appreciated his focus on Holly and me, but when I turned and saw my husband's strained face, I stopped. "Bryce?"

"I'm sorry to interrupt, but I really need to speak with you, Jenna." His voice was thick.

I knew that sound. "What's wrong, Bryce?"

"I'd rather speak to you in private," he urged, tipping his head toward the hall.

"Go on, Jen," Holly said. "We can figure this out. I know Bryce didn't just come in here for nothing. Go take care of whatever it is."

I excused myself and hurried to the hall to join Bryce. He closed the door behind me and asked, "Have you checked your texts?"

"No," I said and took out my phone. "Five missed calls from Becky. What does she want?"

"You need to call her, now."

"Bryce, you're scaring me."

He hugged me, and whispered in my ear, "It's your brother, Jen. I'm so sorry. Becky wanted to tell you."

I was frantic. My heart was stuck in my throat. "Tell me what?" I fumbled with the phone and pressed *Call Back.* Only a few months passed since my scare with Holly. I recently learned the truth once the investigation was closed on Holly's accident. She was hit by a drunk driver who swerved over the line and hit her head on. How could something happen to my brother now? Was he in the hospital? Was it a car accident?

"Jenna," Becky said on the other end.

"What happened?" I nearly screamed into the phone. Bryce rubbed circles over my back and leaned his forehead into the back of my head, and my ponytail. He gripped my shoulders while Becky unfolded the details, loud enough for him to hear.

"It's Mark, Jen. Mark's friend went to the barn."

"What barn, Beck?"

"The one behind the farmhouse where Mark was living. He's been crashing with his friend again. You know how he is. He comes home for a few months and then skips out for weeks on end, never telling anyone where he's going. Well, he got out of rehab last week and moved back in."

"Come on, Becky."

"His friend saw him lying in a pile of loose hay. He thought he was asleep, but when he got closer, he saw his eyes were open and he had no pulse." My sister sobbed. "He's dead, Jen."

I understood what she said, but it didn't feel real. "Was it drugs or what caused him to die?"

"Mom needs us right now." I'm not sure how my mother could handle Holly's problems and Mark's death. I cringed at the thought of how drugs and alcohol changed so many lives in both of these situations. Both were controllable. I've been worried about Mark for a long time. He was detached from those around him and seemed like he was elsewhere, even when he was standing right beside you. He exuded a sense of confidence even though he was always on the run from reality.

"Yeah, well. I'm here with Holly and she is facing enough. I don't think this is the time for me to deliver more bad news." Just like I always did, I mustered up my determination to do what had to be done. I found the grit to keep myself on task. This was a new obstacle and I would conquer it. "Let me go back to the meeting with her physical therapist. I think it would be best if the doctor was there with us when I tell her."

"Good thinking," Becky said.

I hung up and hugged my husband. "I love you."

"I know, Jenna. I love you too. You do what you have to do, but you need to decompress. The kids are home, and they'll need to see you."

"I need to see my mother, too."

Bryce sighed. "I won't argue, but you need to think about you at some point."

"Now is not the time." I returned to the office, closing the door behind me.

"I was just finishing up with your sister, Jenna. It looks like we are going to keep her for a little while longer." The therapist spoke, but I could tell he was taking in my shaken appearance. "Would you like a few minutes alone with Holly?"

"Actually, no. I'd rather you stay."

"Very well," he said.

"What is it, Jen? You look like crap." Holly had a distinct way of expressing herself.

I squatted by her wheelchair and took her hand. "Becky called."

"And?" she pulled away.

"Mark was found dead in his friend's barn."

Holly glanced at the doctor and then spun the wheelchair away from me. "Jesus, what is the point? Why even bother with therapy? It's all so senseless. He never learned. You'd think after all the times he struggled in abusive relationships, addiction, and then losing rights to his children that he would have smartened up. Really? Mark is gone?" Tears welled in her eyes.

I hugged her.

* * *

Alcohol has its way of silencing many struggles. I stopped in to visit my parents before returning home. I could see that my father was silencing the struggles in our family. He was in disbelief that Mark was actually gone. I couldn't wait to get home to Bryce and the kids. The smell of manure and hay made the day melt to the back burner. I wanted to run into the house, put on a pair of comfy leggings and love on my pups. I went to the livingroom where Bryce was waiting with a box of cold pizza and a glass of wine. I took the wine, sipped, and felt an instant relief from the warmth. Just like my father, the struggle was silenced.

Wine had become my go-to for the last several months after Holly's accident. Sometimes it took a smack in the face to realize the apple didn't always fall far from the tree. I just needed to decide if I was an apple following in my father's footsteps, or the pear, because I always knew didn't belong. Knowing that I had Mark's celebration of life to look forward to—and why—I took the wineglass to the kitchen.

"I will not be one of them," I said to Bryce. "This," I raised the glass, "is the reason my father made my

childhood a living Hell. I won't be him and I certainly won't be the role model for our children that he was for me." I dumped the wine down the drain and set the glass on the counter.

Bryce brought his glass over and dumped it out, too. "You know what, Jen? I don't need it either. It's a habit easily replaced with iced sweet tea." He pulled out a pitcher of tea I always kept ready in the fridge and poured it into our wine glasses.

I laughed, "If I make it hibiscus, no one will ever know."

Bryce kissed the top of my head. "It would, but let's keep it to regular tea."

I ate a slice of vegetable pizza without the cheese and went to the bedroom to put on my leggings. I pulled on a hoodie and grabbed a bag of baby carrots from the fridge.

Bryce sat on the arm of the recliner with his hands in his pockets. I noticed he hadn't changed out of his clothes, which meant he was waiting to be the support he thought I needed. But I really wanted to be alone.

"I think I'm going to unwind outside and watch the sun go down. Do you mind?" I asked.

He slid into the seat of the chair and pushed back. "Not at all, but do give me the scoop when you come back."

I snuggled on the comfy couch that overstated our wrap-around porch. The sunset burst with energy behind some wondrous clouds. As I sipped a mug of warm lemon water, I knew I had the support of so many, including the evolving sunset in front of me. I felt that it somehow understood my grief and overwhelming anxiety.

If fear is a choice, why do so many choose it? Why do we remain out of alignment—feeling like we are going against the grain instead of switching directions? We hustle to be superwomen to make us feel safe, but in truth, we are suppressing the inevitable. Eventually, we will have to deal with these fears and overcome them.

* * *

The celebration of life was quick. My brother didn't have a lot of friends. I ordered a slew of butterflies for our family to release in memory of him symbolizing the letting go of the torment of addiction that controlled his life. I wanted to feel his quiet presence and remember his tiny hands reaching for berries too high up in the trees. I visualized his half smile and the safety I felt with him on the school bus near me. Nobody messed with Mark in school!

My mother picked up a couple of Holly's adult kids and brought them to the celebration of life while I stopped by the rehabilitation center to get Holly. Her wheelchair fit in the back of my SUV when it was folded. I wanted to be a supportive daughter to my parents because Becky was a wreck, while Holly was still in disbelief.

Bryce pulled into the handicap spot.

I jumped out, ran to the back, and helped him get the wheelchair. Holly was still in the car and called to us. "Forget it. I'll walk with the walker. I can sit inside. I'm not going to be embarrassed by that damn thing."

"Fine." I grabbed the folded walker with the pull-down seat and hand brakes.

Bryce helped her out of the car and to her feet. There has always been a respect between Holly and Bryce, and I could tell she was comfortable with his help. She stood on her own. Her balance had improved so much with the therapy. I wheeled the walker over to her and she grabbed the handles.

"You're doing great, Holly."

"I still feel like crap," she hissed. She slowly worked her way to the ramp.

I tried not to let her get to me. It was Mark's day. I wouldn't let her attitude take away from the final respects. This was God's plan in action. The sun was shining through the trees and lit up the city. Oddly enough, Mark had a very small insurance policy through the co-op he worked for, and he designated me as the beneficiary. While the policy was tiny, it covered the expense of Mark's cremation, and what was leftover, I split amongst his children.

For after the service, dinner was ready, and I had the memory cards and beautiful butterflies prepped.

I followed my sister; Bryce held my hand. My mother was already there, standing among her grandchildren. When I went in to hug her, I noticed Becky dab the tears escaping her eyes, so I hugged her, too.

There was always a natural divide between my siblings. For me, it was a struggle between living the life that I knew versus pushing toward the life I wanted. Both paths had their own scary points. See, something I realized was that if I had not experienced the childhood my father and mother created, I would not be the person I am today. I was determined, knowledgeable, and resourceful. But I wasn't hardened. I refused to let any of their actions take away the good God had given to me. I had the desire to help people and animals. I loved hard and enjoyed my one life.

It was a shame the rest of them did not always see the fortune that lay before them. They all had opportunities to take a new path. I watched Becky work in the same minimum wage job at a local printing company. She would work every day without any motivation or ability to grow. I tried to help. It took so much for her to trust that she could let go and jump on board with our company outside of what she already knew.

Holly took a seat next to our mother. Becky sat next to her and then I took my seat. Bryce sat in the row behind us. Becky reached for my hand, which reminded me of when she was there for me when I was in school, needing

someone to take me to sporting events or to the mall. It felt awkwardly safe. When we were growing up, our family did not routinely display affection.

I am grateful Becky and I are close.

I loved Mark, and I believed Mark deeply loved our family. Mark didn't know how to release the life that wasn't serving him. There was so much ahead for him, so much unfelt love. As I watched my family members mourn, I got a sense they felt like they were short-changed, robbed of the experience of spending more time with Mark. I wanted to redirect that sadness toward his addiction, the lack of mental healthcare, and his lack of self-love. Mark's soul accomplished what it came to do.

Holly sat quietly, drained from the long day, surrounded by people. She closed her eyes and waited for Bryce to lift her into the backseat. Over the time since the accident, I watched Holly's spirit grow. But I also saw her settle back into her old ways. As her court cases against the impaired driver unfolded, more people gravitated towards her. I often prayed that she would be strong enough to create boundaries and protect herself. I was relieved when she transitioned back home to live with our mother. Mom did so much to help Holly, probably more than she was able to. I watched her endlessly assist with Holly's lawsuit and care. Bryce had recommended a trusted attorney for Holly from his parish men's group, so we knew she was in good hands.

I expected nothing other than an impending lawsuit to attract an increased love from extended family. I decided to focus on my family and the future of my business. It was a changing point in my life. One that allowed me to refocus on the plan I had before the horrible events that took place all those months ago.

Up to this point, I have focused on Holly and the impact her accident had on her and our family. But my story is not complete without learning more about me and my life.

CHAPTER 7

THE
JOURNEY

My childhood did not create a solid foundation for close relationships within my home. Holly was hit or miss. Mark was gone as often as he could manage. Becky was different. She and I had a connection. One that led to her working for Bryce and me with our real estate business. My relationship with my mother, however, was different. I always questioned the validity of her commitments. I wanted to be her advocate; the advocate that would keep her honest and safe. Providing her the dream country-blue kitchen with the geese wallpaper she dreamed of. As a child, I watched her skillfully navigating through all the challenges thrown her way.

I also had a strong relationship with God. A loving God that I read about in the bible. A God that I learned about from the variety of churches that I visited. I remember I trusted this God so much that I began writing letters to him as a teenager. I shared my unfiltered imagination, my hopes, fears and dreams with. I felt so comfortable manifesting where I saw my day, week, year and life going.

I kept my letters in a textured sea-shell linen folder. There was value in all things great and small. The folder was one that I chose because those tiny shells reminded me of his protection. The bible makes numerous references to seashells and for that, the folder had a greater value than any monetary unit.

My heart was so full of the holy spirit. I would have loved my parents' support in the molding of my faith, but it wasn't the way it was supposed to be. I was chosen to voyage out to find it on my own—without boundaries. I was called. I felt it. From a sense of presence, to visions, to full body "holy spirit" goosebumps. I leveraged my friendship with this spirit to push me through a difficult home life, high school obstacles, and encouraging me through college. I found the Catholic college very intimidating because of the rituals and long-standing traditions throughout mass. Attending a Catholic college left me feeling overwhelmed and subordinate to those around me who had been brought up in the faith. The difficulty of paying for the costs of going to college, and the lack of family support, also lead me to feeling overloaded with everything I was trying to do.

I rushed through the process as a marketing major. After taking an introductory class, I was hooked. Getting a business degree made sense to me. It held the promise of a future without having to look into a niche. Marketing came easy. I was used to molding to fit what I wanted to become.

Unlike many other students on campus, I had to work a full-time job which wound up being at a golf store. Since I didn't play golf, learning to sell golf equipment was a new challenge that I sought to master. I learned the industry inside and out—from warranties to sales to vendors. Working at the small golf shop aided in building so many business relationships. Business owners, political parties and retirees who were full of stories would all come in. They always impressed me how this one sport collaborated with so many different people.

My junior year in college was one of the most memorable accomplishments in my academic journey. I received the traditional onyx class ring, which, to date, is one of the most precious items that I own. The ring is a symbol for commitment and promises to uphold the school's values. The ceremony involved the junior class and their families attending a ceremonial mass on campus. The president of the college issued each of us a ring as a sign of achievement. The ring felt so large with the engraving pointed inwards to my heart, patiently waiting to be switched outward upon graduation to face the world. Each of us was going into our senior year, though for me, it would only be one semester untill I completed my college requirements. I skipped the luncheon that was offered by a committee on campus in celebration of the ceremony. I was great at checking the boxes, but had little room for the warm fuzzies.

As a college student, I enjoyed studying and planning at coffee shops. The dark atmosphere and subtle music aided in my concentration. The aroma of the fresh coffee was so enlightening. I was hyper focused on my academics but on the finish line of college, too. While I did have my fair share of fun Panama City Spring Breaks and traditional alcohol-driven bar crawls, I stayed the course. Recognizing the degree of my childhood and beginning to accept my upbringing, I sought out a sliding scale counselor who I saw on a weekly basis. It was here that I learned to regulate my emotions and accept my feelings.

In my senior year, I lived with my sister Becky and her daughter while attending college and working full time. At the time, Becky was a single mother and was grateful for the company and any financial contributions I could help with.

I graduated early from my bachelor's program in January 2002 and began my post college career while my peers were still working on their last semesters. I now wish I would have stayed and enjoyed that final semester of college, but at the time, I felt I needed to keep progressing.

I truly saw college as my gateway to change my family tree. In lieu of my purpose and view, I didn't attend my graduation—nor did I keep up with the peers and friends that I made on campus. I considered them

acquaintances, but we didn't share a camaraderie that allowed me to connect with them on a deeper level. That emotional level was something I never thought anyone would understand, and I didn't have to share my truth that I had hidden behind the curtain. I was there for one thing and that was to graduate and move on to the next step towards success. The longer I attended the college, the more I was influenced by the educated faculty and staff. The tranquility of campus was so peaceful with so many mature trees and carefully placed catholic statues. I saw women with families teaching classes on physics and biology. There were men who taught women writer's courses, and women who were retiring after decades of teaching. I wanted to be like them—knowledgeable and respected.

Earning my degree made me feel accomplished, while others felt it was the next step. For me, it was everything! I will never take for granted all the scholarships that it took to fund the journey and the faith that the school took to accepting an independent student with a crazy background. Receiving my degree gave me opportunities. I wanted to move away from home for my first post college career. Independence was the silver lining to receiving my education, and it was my start on a journey that led me to what my life had become in the years after. I made sacrifices and worked through exhaustion to get to that point and to where I now lived. The journey ahead of me was unraveling all the blessings that were instilled in me. It proved that every heartbreaking moment was a blessing, and every trial was put before me—a lesson to strengthen my convictions and resolve. I understood rejection and received it from a deeper source than a disgruntled customer.

I learned the value behind every dollar spent and the relationships I built, including those with my family. My mother and sisters needed to be in my life. I made peace with my father's actions and would not pass judgment on his influence. For in the bible it says, "Do not judge, and you will not be judged. Do not condemn, and you will not be condemned. Forgive, and you will be forgiven." (Luke 37).

Forgiving someone close to me was easier than one would have thought. I wanted to remain close to my family in heart and proximity but still forge my own path. My father was someone I loved, and to me, love was not something I was willing to throw away. But I was not fooled. I remembered the hardship and neglect. I never forgot the abuse. But that forgiveness gave me the strength to build new relationships and know that they all had their own place and value in my life. I learned to accept what happened to me as a child.

I wound up moving an hour from home in January before graduation to begin my career. I was about to begin my first position that required a college degree. The

company recruited all newly graduated students. Again, I found myself out of the norm. Being hired in January meant I was six months newer than the previous hiring class and would be six months more experienced than the June hiring class. I accepted the difference for what it was. I enjoyed my first job and loved to dabble in the social outings with all the professional young graduates.

In June, several of my work colleagues planned on attending a throwback rock concert called Poison. We all got decked out in faded blue jeans, ripped shirts, tall 80s hair and lots of blue eyeshadow. There were so many of us in attendance, some co-workers who I knew and others that I did not. Several of the songs they played were reminders of the music my older siblings played at home. Lots of drinking was going on at the concert. It was at this concert that I met Bryce.

"Hi, I'm Jenna," I said, hand outstretched, the same way I did while opening any deal.

"Bryce Williams. What department are you in?" he said, grasping mine with the same firm, professional handshake.

It probably seemed cliché, but we hit it off and wound up spending the entire night talking about life and work. It just clicked. This handsome man, with a huge heart, stole mine. We learned each other's music tastes and laughed over the simplest things. His secret passion was agriculture. He absolutely loved farming and all manner of animals. I didn't have that luxury growing up, but I understood running around in fresh grass barefoot, the pureness of cold soil and the beauty of untreated waters and trees.

The concert was a blast. Through the shuffled evening, I somehow got lost from my group. Bryce was a gentleman and gave me a ride home.

Bryce and I started seeing each other outside of work. I learned all about his enormous family that was big on traditions, religion, and the family unit. He had a deep love for his parents and family.

It wasn't until he invited me over for Sunday dinner that I felt that I needed to confess some details of my own. Knowing that perspectives can vary, I didn't want to paint the complete dark picture. The parts that we keep the most private are the ones that we are often the most ashamed of. Growing up, I didn't share anything that I was ashamed of, as I didn't want anyone to feel sorry for me or count me out for a particular situation because of something out of my control.

"I don't think you get it, but . . . I wasn't raised in a traditional family like yours," I said. "My childhood involved leaning on the generosity of people that didn't know me or my family. Don't get me wrong, I'm not looking for pity. There are amazing memories that stick with me to this day." I glanced at him, not knowing what to expect. He sat with his ankle resting on his knee,

holding his coffee cup while I spilled small childhood secrets into the air. "I remember savoring the beauty of mother nature. Taking in the different shapes of the leaves, the various greens in the grass, the coldness of the mud and dirt on my toes brings a smile when I think of doing those things. I loved swimming in natural waters and jumping from the trees." I sighed. "I remember hoping and praying with faith that my imagined future life would come to reality. I remember pushing myself past what might be late expectations to what I believe the thresholds were, such as my clothes having name brand labels and ironing them before a client meeting, because it is important to me. I had none of what you see sitting here before you."

"Jenna, none of that makes me love you any less. I already know you love those things. I see the way your eyes light up when the wind rustles through the trees. You love nature and there is no reason you should feel the need to hide it. And didn't you go to school for marketing? You know how to gain a client."

"Yeah, but there are things like this amazing yellow dress I had. I had an intense appreciation of the mustard yellow dress with big black polka dots, and a cheap plastic belt that I wore until it was officially no more. And it wasn't just the dress. One time, I was a recipient of a neon coat from the local police department. It was a "shop with a cop" campaign and I truly thought that coat was the coolest coat! These were items from strangers because my parents couldn't provide them." And just like that, my smile faded. "My parents had a violent relationship. Mostly my dad to my mom, but she was human. I can't say I fault her because I don't. She reached her breaking point. My mom finally tired and hurting, both mentally and physically. She'd just come home from a late-night shift at the diner. She was still in her uniform, and my father began to rant. It was always something incomprehensible because he was drunk. We weren't fed, and my house was an infested hole no child should have lived in. One night when my father raised his voice, my mother grabbed the iron I had plugged in for my school clothes, and pressed into his chest." I glanced at Bryce. "My mother burned his chest with the hot iron." There was something about that day that felt redeeming. For the first time in my life, I shared my story.

"Your past is your past. Whatever happened was not your fault or fair. But you are stronger for it. It makes me proud to have an independent woman with a vision for her future at my side." Bryce didn't judge me, but I always felt he was trying to make sense of my past, as it was drastically different from his upbringing. He leaned on the table toward me. "You're already writing your own story, Jenna. You have convictions because of your past. It's honorable. I want to introduce you to my family and see what the future has written for us. The past is behind

you. There's no reason to let it destroy the opportunities that lay ahead."

I knew I needed to surrender to my past, but I wasn't sure I was completely ready to do so.

And with that, I went to meet Bryce's mom and his dad. His mom was a peaceful woman with short brown hair. She had a gold cross around her neck, a pair of pearl earrings, and wore a white t-shirt and jeans. His dad was taking the garbage out when we arrived. He called through the open windows to the mom.

"They're here," he said.

I could feel the energy of excitement from his parents as Bryce was their oldest.

She was already at the door when we got out of the car.

"Don't stand out there. Come in. Come in," she said, opening the screen door and standing aside for me to enter.

"Thank you, Mrs. Williams," I said.

Bryce and his father came up behind me. "Mom, Dad, I want you to meet Jenna, the girl I've been telling you about."

His mother gave me the warmest smile. "It is so nice to finally meet you."

"You're even sweeter than he said," his father chided.

They led me to the kitchen, where the white original counter reflected the light from the window in the kitchen. They had a picture of the last supper that hung behind the dining table and plenty of seating for everyone. There was other religious art throughout the home, as well as some construction paper artwork from Bryce's little sister.

"You have a beautiful home," I said. Inside, I was thinking that it was what I always thought our house should have been. The cleanliness, the light, and lack of clutter. There were no elements of a struggling lifestyle. "Is this where you grew up?" I asked Bryce.

"Yup, my father actually had the help of my grandpa to build this home." Bryce proudly exclaimed.

His father grabbed a grape from a bowl of fruit on the island. "I grew up in this town and wanted to raise my family here. My dad was a carpenter and loved the building process. It served its purpose."

"Well, I think it's perfect." I couldn't express how I felt because it made me realize just how different my upbringing was from theirs. I knew I had been raised differently, but never wondered how it would affect my future relationships.

His brother and sister walked through the door and welcomed me into their home with big smiles and hugs. I folded napkins and set the table while Bryce poured glasses of wine. His mother placed a large bowl of spaghetti with homemade tomato sauce in the middle of the table. His father brought a wooden bowl filled

with salad and a platter of sliced Italian bread. As we sat around the table, we immediately said grace. Although I was familiar with the Our Father prayer, it was more of the intention and energy I focused on.

* * *

After several pushes from Bryce to attend mass regularly, I decided to look into a program called RCIA. This program was a step in the direction to learn more about becoming Catholic. When I shared with Bryce that I was joining the program, he was elated. I had no clue if I was ever baptized as a baby. For this reason, I would need to complete a new baptism, first communion and confirmation. Bryce was my sponsor through the program. We attended classes weekly and met a lot of friends along the way. The learning curve and the details felt so big. I enjoyed the smells, lighting, and stillness of the Catholic church. Father Phil conducted all of my sacraments after completing the RCIA program, which took nearly a year.

I could finally say I belonged to a church!

Finding acceptance and a place where I belonged was a lifelong mission that I had not realized I needed or was missing. Bryce urging me to attend opened my eyes to the traditions and values that I grew to love. Many times,

I found myself getting lost in the liturgy. My spirit found a home and I found peace.

CHAPTER 8

NEW BEGINNINGS

It was 2004 and I was still dating Bryce. My family loved Bryce. I was careful with this as I wanted to be sure it was for the right reasons.

For one of our dates, Bryce took me to the county fair. In our county, it consisted of 4-H shows with goats, pigs, sheep, and cattle. There were some chickens, roosters, and a few small animals in cages, and a display of vegetables that kids had grown. There was also an old wooden building that looked like it had been a paddock at one time. Entrants contributed a craft to be judged at the fair. There were pies, cookies, cakes, and crocheted blankets as well as terrariums and soldered sculptures.

The night we went, there was a corn shucking contest and a magic show. Bryce grabbed us lemonades, a deep-fried onion, and some salt potatoes. Going to the fair had been on my wish list for us for quite some time, but we couldn't seem to get there with our busy lives. This time, we made it happen. He made sure the night was perfect. We rode the Ferris wheel and the merry-go-round. I laughed when he tried to climb around the front of the horse while it was moving up and down because he nearly lost his grip. I reached to grab his arm to keep him from falling and almost fell off my own. After that, we got a huge pink cotton candy and shared it as we sat in the audience while the magician was introducing his assistant.

We applauded each time she went to curtsy because he would find a new gadget or string of handkerchiefs from her bonnet or ear. I watched Bryce's face light up with each corny act. I loved the simplicity of the show, yet the cunning in which it was pulled off was far from simple. The guy was fantastic and funny. We picked at the cotton candy through the performance.

When it was over, I went to wash my hands. Bryce waited for me by the grandstand. It was the last night of the fair, which always ended with an enormous fireworks display. As a child, our family often ventured to the county fair. We would "find a ride" to get dropped off at the fair, in which we would stay until my mother's shift ended at the diner so we could catch a ride home with her. After I went to college, I forgot about the small country fairs and their allure. And now, here I was with Bryce, and it was as much fun as I remembered. Just as I reached Bryce, the first firework exploded. It was red and green sparklers that seemed to go higher and higher with cracks and pops and booms.

Bryce tapped me on the shoulder, but I didn't want to look away. "Jen," he said. He was standing behind me.

"What's up?" I asked, turning to look at him.

"This," he said. He snapped his fingers next to my ear and pulled out a square diamond on a white gold band.

I couldn't help but smile. It was corny and sweet, and the ring was exactly what I had told him over a year before, what I would love to have. He remembered. "Bryce?"

"Ms. Jenna Carlson, would you do me the honor of being my wife?"

The next firework went off, so I shook my head 'yes' and kissed him. He slid the ring on my finger, and we watched the display with his arms wrapped around me. I kept feeling the diamond with my thumb. It was surreal and yet humbling. I was the type of woman who loved being a country girl, and the finest things in life, and Bryce got that.

* * *

We were to get married in April of the following year. It should have been the most glorious day of my life, but it turned into an event that would send my anxiety spinning out of control.

The first event that hit me was when we decided to marry in the same Catholic church Bryce began attending after he returned home from graduating college. I did not have a church to call my own, but I attended the Baptist church in town or the Catholic parish periodically on campus. When Bryce started bringing me to his services, it was new and exciting, but the traditions scared me. There were so many repetitive prayers. I found that same college feeling of intimidation because of the rituals of the catholic faith. But we wanted a traditional Catholic wedding. And to boot, we were trying to conserve finances because we were paying for our wedding ourselves. At the time, I was balancing my career at a non-profit, completing my MBA and planning our wedding.

Family support wasn't something I could count on. We did not celebrate marriage in my family—it simply meant you were committed to that one person. My family found this same commitment through simply having children with a partner. I truly believed my different lifestyle also intimidated my family. I remember telling my father my plans for a wedding and he scoffed it off. My brother once called me one evening asking for money to pay an attorney. After receiving my no, he said I needed to spend more time helping my family. Bryce and I had been together for two years before the engagement.

The wedding planning began as a playbook. I had to look at my family lineup to see who I could ask to fill the spots for the bride's side. We asked my niece and nephew to make their debut as flower girl and ring bearer. I carefully chose substitutes to fill all roles for a traditional Catholic wedding mass. My mother was coping with an alcoholic husband whose health was quickly declining.

Becky was struggling to make ends meet. My father felt a lot of shame for not being able to help pay for my ceremony.

Though we planned, it didn't stop my worry. I had no idea how my family was going to act as the day grew closer. I wanted them there. They were all invited, but the only ones I could talk to with confidence were my mother and Becky. My father didn't want to take part in the day.

I had to accept that he had his own reasons, even if I didn't know what they were. I came to realize that his intention of not wanting to take part in the ceremony hurt more than him not actually doing so. Why wouldn't a father want to support his daughter?

As I grew more accomplished, I would sometimes hear my father take credit for my success in conversations with his family. In some respects, maybe he did push me. Maybe it was all the conversations of how he could have done better. Or maybe it was the none of this really matters mentality that lowered expectations.

I confided my fears to Bryce. I didn't know how his family and the parish would feel about my own parents not fully taking part in the day. At this time, I worried how others perceived my father's absence. I felt it made me less worthy of enjoying the celebration.

I wanted to believe Bryce that everything was going to be okay, but I struggled with trust. Whenever I thought someone was going to be there for me—I was forgotten. Forgotten to be picked up, forgotten to pay back candy bar fundraising money or forgotten to grab a white cheer turtleneck. Meeting Bryce gave me a glimpse of what life should have been like—organized and structured. During this time, I clenched onto the organization and structure that my soul craved, but I failed to find the peace, freedom, and natural flow I was searching for. My heart was not open during this planning period to receive the grace needed—it was all about survival.

* * *

I wore a modest dress with a white mother-of-pearl bodice and a long, flowing skirt. Bryce waited for me at the altar dressed in a dark three-piece suit. His parents sat in the front pew while my mother sat with Becky. I emerged in the doorway and spotted the man I chose to spend the rest of my life with and realized how lucky I was. He winked at me when the music started.

My brother-in-law walked me down the aisle. My father did not attend my wedding.

But our priest, Father Phil, knew exactly how to handle every moment. The ceremony was flawless. Bryce lifted my veil and the moment I looked into his eyes; I knew we were meant to be. We said our vows, which to me, probably held a deeper meaning than most people. I had personally seen vows erode with my parents.

After the kiss, which felt like the first, I was giddy and relieved at the same time. I had just leaned into a fear of hosting such a sacred ceremony. I was about to change my family history. I got married in my mid-twenties. I wasn't living at home with a child and relying on substances to get by. I wasn't working myself sick either. Bryce and I had an amazing future mapped out—careers, financial freedom and eventually children. We worked for everything we had, and the wedding was now a part of us.

It really was our big day.

As I look back, I guess it was better that my father hadn't shown up. Bryce and I opted to have an open bar at the reception because many of our friends and his family enjoyed a cocktail hour. Nearly every event that we attended family or social included alcohol. We were social people- we could predict the people that would over drink during our reception. It's interesting how we can accept some people overindulging and others we cannot. Some can quickly label people as having a drinking problem while the people that are labeling routinely enjoy their own cocktails nightly. It's all perspective. Many people in my family drank out of habit. I had seen their behaviors switch from cordial to crazy. I was not prepared to deal with the craziness of my family's drinking that night, especially if my father would have attended.

Anyway, Bryce and I had our first dance, followed

by the mother-son dance. My brother, Mark, made a presence at the wedding reception- almost a controlled presence. Something about it will never leave my mind. He disappeared as often as he could. I'd like to say that I knew he would show up for my wedding, but to be honest, I wasn't sure. He tried his best to escape our home life in any way that he could.

Mark was an amazing brother when he wanted to be. He, like the rest of us, endured the darkness and hunger, but he fell victim to the draw of drugs and alcohol. First, he would share a joint with one of his friends at school, Ricky. I never liked him much. He talked Mark into skipping school on the few days he did g,o and had him smoking weed outside the convenience store next door while ducking behind the brick façade, careful not to get caught. The teachers used to do a look-around before going inside. Ricky and Mark would laugh about it when they hung out.

Mark was set in his ways—always willing to put up a fight for what he believed in, both at home and at school. He loved to dance and to draw, but still had that side of mischief. He was an old soul that fought many obstacles in his path. I've come to realize that these obstacles weren't blocking his path- they were simply part of it.

My stringy red head pulled herself up the ladder and out of Hell through grit and hard work. Yet I was still nervous about how my family would act and was

reminded of the severity because we chose to have an open bar.

Luckily, my siblings and mother understood. They ended up having a great time. Dancing barefoot—requesting music from the DJ and watching their kids take part in our big day. I was grateful to have my mother at the wedding and reception. My mom saved the day as she usually does. She looked wonderful in a royal blue dress and curly hair. I could tell she was so nervous during the ceremony. She cried several times, tears of happiness. During the reception, she made sure the catering was done correctly, and the cake was perfect. She was the first to arrive at the reception and the last to leave.

CHAPTER 9

A NEW KIND
OF LOVE

I interviewed with several pharmaceutical companies trying to gain a sales position. I had the know-how and the education to back it, but it was a tough industry to break into. Still, I endured until the right fit opened their doors. The pharmaceutical industry offered prestige, great pay and a lot of perks, and I wanted to be part of it. During a three-step interview with a company that I was really interested in, I found out the position I was interviewing for was filled by another candidate. Oddly enough, one of the managers during the interview process was from my hometown. He noted I would do great there if I was willing to relocate an hour from where Bryce and I lived, which was farther away from Bryce's family. Bryce agreed to make this sacrificial move. The position wound up being one I loved, and I stayed with them for over ten years. Sales always afforded me the freedom to set schedules based on my time and travel. I liked traveling, especially to places that I had never been, even in my home state. And at the core of my love for the position was the fact that the position allowed me to work in my hometown—and that felt very good. I was comfortable there.

Bryce and I relocated into a great neighborhood and into a beautiful home. We had financial freedom and enjoyed life. During this time, my father's health was seriously declining. From his heart to diabetes and finally his liver. Because my sales territory wasn't far away, I could visit with my father frequently. I recommended local physicians that I trusted to my mom to care for my dad. My mother would share all the details of each specialist appointment. There were so many tests and so many more medicines. My father was noncompliant as a patient. He still drank alcohol to the very end. After depleting his time in hospice, they admitted my father to the hospital. My mother sat by his side every step of the way. I wondered if this is what the vow meant—in sickness and health. Was this man ill his entire life? Mom stayed by his side.

My father wound up passing away in his sleep.

His death created an opening for my mother to focus on herself. We became closer than we ever were. I envisioned my mother, Becky, and me being the three Musketeers. Holly was back working in HR for a trucking company and still relied on our mom for bathing and cooking. We would often think back to all the times my dad was incarcerated. All the girls in the house came together to make it work when he was away. From DUI charges to driving without a license to domestic abuse— the lists were endless. Each time, we would figure something out and move on.

A year later, Bryce and I welcomed our first child. I read every book on how to be a mom! I tracked the size of the embryo and used a heart rate monitor to make sure the heartbeat was still viable. There were books on parenting, and I absorbed every word. Something I hadn't thought of was the reactions of others to my returning to work after the baby was born. I was a professional woman with a full-time career. I had responsibilities outside of my home. Traditionally in Bryce's family, the women stayed home to manage the house and their children. In my family, even outside of my immediate home, the women worked. They had to.

I remember wanting and needing to work, but worried about what my husband's family would think. I would cringe when asked how short my maternity leave was or if I thought I was going back to work after the baby was born. Work was an outlet for me. I enjoyed the freedom and the responsibility. Just because I was becoming a mother didn't mean I had to give up that part of my life. A part that took years to build. The guilt filled my gut because it felt wrong to want both a child and a career. I invested thousands of dollars into my education and was reaping the benefits while investing in a future for my children. That was an opportunity my parents did not have, nor did they know how to achieve for any of us.

There was so much more to living in Starke County, the most impoverished in the state of Indiana. Yes, I remember staying in lots of hotel rooms paid for by my dad, when he worked, or by the Red Cross when the bayou flooded us out of our home. But I also remember swimming. It felt free to just run and jump into the crystal-clear water and sit on downed trees. There were no rules in the bayou. Though the Red Cross provided not only hotel rooms, but they also provided sandbags, food, and monetary resources when the floods came. It was like winning the lottery for our family. Excitement filled my siblings and I because there were usually amenities that weren't always guaranteed. We had a hotel with a pool and air conditioning. That worry wort in me didn't have to worry about adult things such as unsafe or faulty wiring, leaks or utilities.

With our mother working and our father incarcerated, we had unlimited freedom to canoe or swim in the bayou. It was where we found peace. I still recall the pure sound, sight, and smells of the uncontaminated water and trees. It was a glimpse of life where time seemed to stand still. It was rare for us to have reliable transportation. Becky's friends or boyfriend would generally give me a ride to school functions.

And just like after Dad died, Becky and mom had to leverage time. In our youth it was for me to go to activities and such, then it was for Becky to take her daughter to the same events she had to chauffeur her me to. Back when I was adamant about a ride, my mother relied on

her second uncle, who was always around. He was in our life, but I never felt comfortable around him. He would provide cigarettes and alcohol as we got into our teen years and then transportation or money. After his so-called generosity, he would always complain about providing charity and giving handouts.

I would always cry so hard when I had to stay at his house and would try to stay awake all night. While I was never one of his subjects, I wondered if any of my family members were. I didn't trust him or his intentions. Trust was hard to earn. I relied a lot on my intuition in getting to know someone. If it came down to it, I'd have given up my career in a heartbeat to prevent one of my children from feeling the angst I had to overcome.

In a way, I was lucky. Bryce traveled with his medical device company, so it often left me home alone with Meghan. We balanced my travel with Bryce's travel and my mother's availability. I quickly learned the ins and outs of the coined phrase work-life-balance. I was known to have had my husband and newborn travel with me to meetings or coordinate shipping breast milk to Bryce for our baby. I always made it work so that my family was first. As my career progressed, I was honored when newer representatives would reach out on maternity leave benefits and work life strategies.

I did it well, and I enjoyed it!

During my employment with the pharmaceutical

company, Bryce and I welcomed two additional children, Ben and Zach. They all attended an amazing Baptist Church Daycare Ministry. We had the best for them because, in reality, I felt our children were the most important assets in our lives. I loved them with a fire in my heart that burned so hot, I could not fathom how my parents didn't find a way to foster what made each of my siblings tick. Bryce and I thoroughly loved their daycare and considered the tuition paid an investment into our children's futures.

* * *

Around 2014, Bryce and I decided we were going to general contract our own house on ten acres. We had four kids and were selling our home to move into a rental. The plan seemed great on paper, but when we downsized to a small rental, I found myself second guessing our decision. Bryce orchestrated the design of the house for our current family size and financial status. In the process, he felt the calling to start a business, since we were so financially comfortable. I reluctantly signed for our LLC. That was a tough time for me. With Bryce and I both working full time, starting a business, and raising four kids, building a custom home seemed ridiculous. There were many nights where we sat on the fire escape while the kids slept, and we questioned what we were thinking, but we never questioned whether we

bit off more than we could chew. There were obstacles, yes, but we never let that stop us before. And we would not let them stop us now when we had four young people watching and learning from everything we did.

Not to mention, all our coworkers thought we were crazy because the kids were each starting to have their own activities. Not more than a year later, we began our home-building journey. I struggled with all the details and juggling to finalize the planning of the house. There were permits and certificates of occupancy. There were contractors, construction draws, and so much insurance. We also had to choose furniture, trim, hardware, and decide on the size of the barn we wanted. Ten acres was enough to have everything we dreamed of, and it allowed for the hobby farm we wanted.

One evening after we bought the property, I walked out to the tree line where we planned to build a barn after the house was finished. The sun was setting, shining through the darkened tree trunks, and then illuminating the limbs. I could imagine walking the yard of this country setting feeling all that God had created. Bryce was standing behind me.

"You see those stars, Babe?" he said.

I looked up in awe. No matter how many times I looked up, the universe inspired me. It was vast and limitless, just like life. I knew there were no limitations when there was so much more than our small corner of Indiana. "It's beautiful. Can you imagine coming out here, sitting by a fire pit, wrapped in blankets, and just staring up into that amazing sight?"

"We closed on the property today. That means we can do whatever we want. If you desire a fire pit, then I can't see why we need to wait." He wrapped his arms around me and nestled into my neck.

"I love you, Bryce. You never stop getting me."

"We have four kids together and invested in a future farm. I hope I get you." He laughed, "Can you picture us in a big house, sitting on a wraparound porch, sitting in matching rocking chairs when we're old and the kids are gone?"

"Now that you mention it, yeah. I can." And I did. He always wanted a farm, and I always wanted a full life, one that included Bryce, my kids, and whatever additions we could bring in. Bryce and I shared the country life upbringing—albeit two different levels of country. I was raised rurally mostly between moves with domestic animals and Bryce was all 4H.

* * *

It was a busy year, but our home was built. There was still so much to do from landscaping to barns. We hired out everything in the house from roofing to electrical to cosmetic. We quickly learned so many ins and outs within the process such as making sure lien waivers were

signed when a job was complete and before you paid the contractor. The kitchen had oak cabinets and tongue in groove hardwood that ran throughout the main floor. Upstairs, the bedrooms had plush carpet and marble tile in the bathrooms. Each bedroom had a conjoining bathroom. I was a firm believer in the kids each having their own space. We made sure the plan allotted for a home office because the real estate business that we started was really starting to take off.

When we finished the house, the children were ecstatic because they officially had their forever home. The ability to provide this home for them filled me with so much peace. Our business was growing at the same junction as our lives. All was good, and to make it even better, I woke up one morning knowing I was pregnant. We welcomed our fourth child that summer and named her Hope. Shortly after Hope was born, the pharmaceutical company that I worked for began to downsize and they offered me a severance package. Though I was happy, it seemed that my life had reached a point that I would say was overwhelming. It was good, but sometimes, it was easy to lean on a glass of wine to numb the craziness. I realized no matter the environment, alcohol was used to the same degree, either it be celebrations or casually. It didn't discriminate. It was at this time that I made the decision that I wasn't going to be like my parents, or family, or dear friends again. I was okay being different.

I decided alcohol couldn't play a part in my life at all, no matter what. Family functions and dinners with friends felt so different without alcohol. Alcohol has its way of being the elephant in the room, causing many poor decisions.

With Bryce's support, I decided I wanted a healthier lifestyle. I omitted alchohol first followed by meat. I learned to lean on the flavors and the generally good feeling of an organic vegan lifestyle over that of meat and alcohol. It was a big switch, but my body felt better for it, and my anxiety lessened.

I truly believed my dietary changes played a big part in my mental stability. I learned to love myself and accept the ups and downs. My children were blessings I cherished, and I felt free being able to snuggle with them, knowing that they were growing up with the full understanding of what it meant to be loved—what it meant to have contentment and stability.

CHAPTER 10

GROWTH

After 2017, our real estate business completely took off. We started by flipping houses and building a rental portfolio. We learned about passive income years before but didn't feel the time was opportune for giving it the proper devotion we knew it would take. In fact, when Bryce and I started, we never expected to leave our mainstream jobs. It was risky and there were no givens. We grew with a partnership of a franchise and several masterminds to teach us the art of what we wanted to achieve. Bryce and I had organically grown our business and personally had sat in each seat for our company—Bryce more operationally and I focused more administratively.

We decided to grow our team and culture. We brought on investors. We took both additions to heart. We found that all our team members and our investors personally believed in us. They had faith in our abilities to make a return on their investments.

Our business danced with several partnerships. Having the marketing knowledge backing me along with the financial and investment understanding from my

MBA proved that my education had been a worthwhile long-term investment. With our careers, we learned to read the room. To know when a buyer was ready to walk or when a seller was at the lowest acceptable offer. The ebb and flow of working alongside my spouse created the perfect work life balance. We had created an amazing team eventually including my sister Becky who we brought on board when we needed more hands-on deck. The business grew to where we employed several people with great revenue. Becky was the first voice customers heard when they called our business. She has the same likability that my mother had from working in restaurants. She connects with sellers easily when they share why they are selling their house even if it is out of the box. Again, she and I were raised out of the traditional box.

I was so happy to see Becky leave her previous company, a local printing company. She felt stagnant and not encouraged to grow and step into her light. I knew she had a voice inside of her—and it was so awesome to hear her use it. I quickly encouraged her to join our company executive team that met every Thursday. She could give her insights with conviction. Customers and the rest of our team loved Becky coming on board. And I loved the ability to pull her along- because I knew what she had inside- a big heart!

It was great seeing my sister believe in herself and

take on a role that allowed her to respect herself. I could see the pride she felt and saw it when she helped a customer with a difficult situation. My sister was just learning what it felt like to achieve success.

I could see the feeling of success and fulfillment when Becky's daughter graduated high school and was bound for college. Becky and I generated ideas for her senior open house, toured several colleges and eagerly awaited the fall when my niece would start her freshman year at the same college that I attended.

Success is achieving a goal. I want to believe that my sister, Holly, achieved some form of success and that she is happy.

For Becky and my niece, I knew they were on a road to success because they already accomplished so many goals. From filling out college applications to deciding which college to attend. My niece was so fortunate to have my sister along her side. I always craved that same support when I was in her shoes. I dreamed of wearing the college sweatshirt just to realize that college wasn't for me. My niece did it, and my sister did too! Selfishly, I realized being the different one in my immediate family was actually an example for future generations—one to follow.

After I left the pharma company, I felt the same shock that my mom felt leaving her restaurant work. I felt a sense of attachment in my work, because it took so much energy. I noticed I spent a lot of my energy trying to prove to others that I was enough. I hadn't yet reached the point where I felt I was worthy enough, just as I was. I was always chasing the manifestation that hitting the next goal would make me better valued. No matter the size of the goal—it would prove to someone outside of me I was enough.

* * *

"I need to work. I've always worked. If I don't, what will I do?" said my mother one afternoon.

"Maybe you've worked enough, Ma," I said. "You weren't the one throwing beer cans and passing out on the couch, missing your shifts. You hustled every day. Maybe it's your time to accept that your body has had enough."

Our mother no longer worked outside of the home. She traded the energy from work and instilled it into taking care of Holly—from bathing, food prep and errands. Secretly, I think she finds fulfillment in feeling needed. Additionally, she was caring for one of Holly's grandchildren. Crazy how this world works out. Mom now has an opportunity to shield a little lady from a negative household through the foster care system. The same shielding I always prayed for. It came at just the right time.

Holly can now work full time. She still works for the

same employer that she did during her accident. They were so supportive of her during her recovery. Holly is blessed that my mom will never leave her side. I always wonder if Holly realizes what a true blessing the outcome of the accident was. The opportunity to defeat all odds— from death to the inability to walk. I feel blessed to have experienced a miracle in front of me with her recovery.

It was too late for Mark, and in a way, I felt guilty about that. I wondered if I told him enough or at all that I loved him. He was always very dark and distant. His children live on, and we are blessed to see them on holidays and celebrations. They have children of their own now. I know he would have loved them dearly.

Because of all the cards I was dealt, I learned how to live a rich, fulfilling life. Not rich in finances, but in living. Every memory and triumph led to me standing in the barn with my four children. I am a forty-three-year-old mother in overpriced leggings and an old barn coat, with a pair of rubber boots, sitting in the hay inside the barn built by her husband's hands, painted by hers. And why was I in the hay? Because the miracle of life was evolving. The beautiful long black eyelashes of the tiny life emerged from her mother's womb. Bryce helped the mom with a pull of the calf's legs and smiled at the tiny face and pink tongue.

My daughter, Meghan, kissed the mamma's head while my youngest son, Zach, brought her a warm towel.

Ben held his sister, Hope, and whispered, both smiling. Bryce squatted beside me, rubbing a cotton rag over the newborn's nose.

One month later

Word of my life story got out. I gave talks at high schools on career day but was also asked to go to women's groups as a guest speaker. I knew women had a preconceived notion about self worth and accepting their childhood—like really accepting it. Seeing me dressed professionally walking into an auditorium seemed out of touch. So, I took to taking the microphone at the start of every speech and repeating the one phrase that summed up stereotypes, "I'm done pretending." The audience would grow silent as I told the story of how I got to where I was. Many women came up to me afterwards, asking how I got to where I was. I told them by making peace with my past and healing past hurts.

Unbeknownst to me, this resonated deep within the women's groups and because of that resonance, I found myself standing on the stage at a local university, gripping a wooden podium, staring into a sea of graduates. I was the keynote speaker. This time, when I spoke into the microphone, I had a harder, more detailed message; one that took years for me to realize. I told them the story about overcoming abuse, neglect, and poverty. But I also told them about my farm, and the blessing of seeing my

children's faces reflect true joy at the miracle I held in my hands. "You see," I said, "that moment reinforced my belief that you can never give up on your dreams. You are created with a blueprint of all that you need to succed. Your past has brought you here and your determination and faith will take there. Be the one to choose your destiny. I chose mine—I wouldn't change a thing."

EPILOGUE

My name is Mandy Hull, the author of the story you just read. There are a multitude of reasons for putting this story in your hands. First, it was to put aside the assumption that all success comes easy. Much like the main character, Jenna Williams, I endured a life of poverty, an unattractive family tree, and abuse. And just like her, I learned that your mind must be strong so you can push through whatever God puts before you. Fear is simply an indicator of something that you need to overcome. The good news is that everything that you need to overcome your fears is already inside of you. Dream without limits!

Your thoughts will become your reality, so it's important to choose them wisely. Through journaling, meditating and a healthy lifestyle, you can find your inner peace. Everyone has obstacles in their life that they are working on healing. Keep in mind that these obstacles aren't holding you back from your dreams- they are simply guiding you to the right path to your dream. The goal is to never give up on your dreams. It is that resilience which will help them come to life, creating the destiny that you choose.

I also feel that it's important to note that I see the other side of receiving; I see the giving. The giving of presents during holidays, the food donations during our kids' food drives at school, and the giving of myself to others. It is a quality I wanted to give to Jenna. Something that made her the voice she became. See, Jenna's story hasn't ended, it's still being told.

As a 43-year-old mom, Jenna ends up teaching her children about the importance of a positive mindset, has a strengthened relationship with her mother and creates a local shoe bus to give back to the community with her sister. She empowers women daily through speaking engagements and podcasts. She leads women to healing past traumas that are holding them back from their passions and goals. There is peace in finding yourself-your true self. A view I share with Jenna.

Because of her strong advocacy for embracing the professional and personal sides of a mother's life, she became a national speaker. It is possible to have what you want, and it's okay to want something for yourself. Just as I learned in my own life, you don't have to be Super Mom. You can want your own business and to have an expensive latte for no reason other than you want to enjoy the sweet foam. It's an indulgence that does not need to give way to guilt. My mother stood up to my father, just as Jenna's did to hers. Life should not come to ultimatums and abuse. You can't be the abuser to yourself, either. If the bills are paid and the children are well cared for, then take a moment to see what you need for yourself. Sometimes the answer is simply to be seen as more than an extension of the kids or the other half of your spouse.

One way to be seen is to go against the grain. Hence the title I chose for this book. From the start, we are taught to dress, act, eat, and even perform in a certain way. Be bold and take a risk. No portfolio is larger than the one you create on yourself.

I always say, "Strive for freedom and peace. Fitting in doesn't matter." It's true. I live in the country, and I embrace going barefoot. I actually prefer it. The purity of the natural resources the universe gives to us is a gift. Realize that not all gifts are wrapped in pretty bows. Sometimes it is an act of kindness, and others a teachable moment. Those moments that affect us negatively are lessons we are learning. Stop and ask yourself what it is about the moment that is triggering for you and why. Nature is your friend! Go for a walk in the woods—stop and listen. Take the time to appreciate every little thing in your life. Make time for the children, and teach them everything you know, but don't be afraid to learn from them. Knowledge is ever changing.

Personally, I raised my kids to be able to bloom wherever they are planted. They can eat at the finest restaurants and help birth a calf. I want them to know

how to punch a time clock and how to manage money. I am the mom who has snotty tissues in her designer bag and am proud to see my kids running around in muck boots and bathing suits. I'm not afraid to get dirty myself. Yes, I like getting mani-pedi's, but I also enjoy running through sun showers and swimming in the bayou.

I gave Jenna my mantra, "I'm done pretending." This is a recurring theme through the story and how she alludes back to being a grounded mom who is also a woman. She is the result of determination and vision. She shares that passion and puts it out to the community in different ways. Many people don't realize that you can start a fundraiser, food drive, or scholarship with minimal effort. If you have excess, you can teach others about your journey. Just as I have shared with you, the reader, through Jenna.

Another message I want you to take away from this story is to dream crazy big. I embrace our kids dreaming crazy big and love that they are willing to share them. I always had vivid dreams. I dreamt of my future, and I saw them come to life. I wanted to go to a prestigious college, and I did. Dreams are as real as we want them to be. And that means not forcing unnecessary decisions on my kids. I don't want my kids to feel they have to decide between being a parent or doing what they love. I found out you can do both!

I will be the first to tell you I wear expensive leggings

to cattle shows and my husband thinks I'm crazy when I do. My husband dreamt of being a farmer, but had the call to go into real estate. By doing both, he can be a hobby farmer with our family at his side. I love every moment of our country life!

Our kids go to great schools and I'm a vegan who doesn't eat meat but owns a cattle farm. I've sprayed Tire Shine on a livestock trailer and still turn my hands purple from eating berries. I don't pretend to fit in, and I didn't raise my kids to fit in either. From my experience I have found a true balance between filling my cup so I can help others fill their cup. It took some time for me to realize that by me stepping into my light and accepting me for me, I then invite and encourage others to do the same.

Just like when I was a little girl existing in infested living conditions, I was always aware of my human side. I was just looking for freedom and a little bit of peace, running into the field, staring into the wild blue yonder— the vast world beyond my small piece of Heaven.

I still look out at that same big open sky.

ABOUT MANDY HULL

Mandy grew up grounded in nature, nestled in a rural community. She experienced the changing of seasons, the splash of streams and bayous, bare feet in wet grass and passed time examining all that the big sky had to offer. All the nature experience was simply an avenue to suppress the abuse within her parental homestead, from domestic to alcohol and the lack of essential care. She mastered the art of repressing the negative and ran albeit, *against the grain*, of normalcy within her family to what society called success by conquering college education to a master's level and starting a traditional family and a successful business.

While Mandy had obtained academic and surface level awareness to serve others and the world—she lacked true self-awareness. She began a journey of self-discovery by looking within at the cause and effect of reactions—including to the depths of all that she avoided from her upbringing. The remembering process answered a lot of questions and opened wounds that needed to be worked through and healed.

Mandy is still on her journey of self-discovery, and she hopes to be an inspiration to others on their journey.

www.ingramcontent.com/pod-product-compliance
Lightning Source LLC
Chambersburg PA
CBHW051514260626
47162CB00008B/2959